KNIGHT'S *Haven*

Book One of Knights of KSI Series

BY SHELLEY JUSTICE

KNIGHT'S HAVEN

Caution to Readers: This book is intended for readers ages 18+. The story contains foul language, violence, sexual content, and death of a loved one.

Cover Design: CT Cover Creations

Cover Photo: Cover'd by 6:12 Photography

Editor: Write Right Edits

Formatter: Dee's Busy Bee Formatting

ISBN: 979-8-9857177-9-2 (ebook)

979-8-9912527-0-6 (paperback)

Dedication

I dedicate Knight's Haven to the memory of my mother, my biggest fan who always believed in me and knew I would succeed in achieving my dream before I even knew it myself. I love you, Momma, and I miss you every day.

Chapter One

Amazing how one phone call could implode my life so completely.

The thought bounced around Katarina Walsh's mind as she sipped her coffee, the bitter flavor lingering on her tongue. She savored the warmth as it traveled down her throat and spread through her belly. Her stomach rumbled, reminding her of the delectable stack of pancakes resting on the table in front of her. Though she was famished, she refused to rush her breakfast. It was a last-minute splurge, depleting the few dollars she had left in her bank account.

After a restless night spent in her car, shivering from the hint of fall clinging to the air, she'd decided to treat herself. She might regret it later, if her job leads didn't pan out. But for now, she would enjoy every sip and every last bite.

The diner's business was starting to pick up. Kat had arrived early and claimed a back booth before the place filled with customers. The last thing she wanted was to draw attention. Her clothes were rumpled, her hair limp and in need of a wash. She hadn't bothered with make-up since she was planning to be on the road in a short while. If her mother could see her now, she would be appalled.

Her mother's image filled her mind's eye, bringing a sad smile to her lips. Lori Walsh always believed in putting her best foot forward. Her hair was always perfectly coiffed, her clothes pressed and immaculate, her nails manicured, her makeup subtle enough to highlight her features without being overly dramatic. Lori was a lovely woman without all the fuss, but she would never step foot from the house, even to retrieve the mail from the box by the curb, without putting some effort in her appearance.

Even before she was left jobless and became a nomad, Kat hadn't put much stock in her appearance. Her job as a computer programmer had allowed her to dress somewhat casually, and her hair was cut in an easy-to-maintain style that often meant being thrown into a ponytail. Since she wore glasses to read, she wore little makeup so as not to have it rub off on her lenses. Kat was more about convenience and comfort than style, but even she had reached a whole new level in the last few months.

She pulled herself from her memories as customers began to filter in. She smiled at the group of older gentlemen who gathered at tables at the front, obviously old friends who broke bread together on a regular basis. *Every town has a ROMEO club*, she thought, recalling her mother's acronym for "Retired Old Men Eating Out."

The two waitresses flitting between the tables wore black aprons over their simple tops and jeans, athletic shoes providing support for their feet. The way they greeted each customer as if he or she was family and hustled their orders out to them spoke of years of experience. The closer the clock ticked to 7:30 a.m., the more business professionals made an appearance, wearing everything from collared shirts and khakis to tailored business suits. The diner seemed to be a popular place, but a brief drive through the town had revealed to Kat the diner was the only place open for breakfast.

She'd never planned to stop in the quaint little town of Grayson Cove and certainly never meant to spend as much time here as she had. Something about the small town with its surprisingly bustling activity had drawn her to stay and explore before moving on. The last odd job she'd picked up before continuing her job search had yielded enough money to linger for a bit. She made her dollars stretch farther by opting to sleep in her car rather than stay in a cheap motel or a bed and breakfast.

Nothing about her life right now followed any kind of plan. When she was on the fast track to a promising and lucrative career, she never considered a diner breakfast special an extravagance. Then she'd gotten the phone call from her brother with news of their mother that turned her world topsy turvy.

The phone call seemed like a lifetime ago. She shouldn't be dwelling on it now, but the memories refused to lie dormant. She woke from fitful sleep thinking not of the mother who counseled her through her teenage years but of the mother whose memory and personality were stolen by the dementia. The independent and put-together Lori Walsh could no longer be trusted to live on her own, prompting Kat to leave the job she loved and move home to care for her mother.

The first couple of years had been tough enough, with Kat working from home so she could watch after Lori. Most days, her mother was the same Lori Walsh who knew how to breathe sunshine into the worst days. The days where her mother could barely remember her name and could never recall who her daughter was cast a foreboding cloud over those two years, but those days numbered only a few.

If only their life could have stayed that way. If only the dementia wouldn't have taken more of Lori Walsh's mind. If only it hadn't become necessary for Kat's brother to sell their childhood home to cover the expense of the long-term care facility where her mother now lived. It was the *if onlys* that kept Kat twisted in knots, that kept her on the road searching to regain the life she'd willingly given up for her mother.

She shouldn't focus on that now. It was time to move on from Grayson Cove. This had been her third town in which to job search since leaving her home in Evergreen. She thought the search would be easy, and considering how her first job landed unexpectedly in her lap, she was a bit surprised she'd not had similar luck this time around. Especially when the IT job market was hot right now.

Kat raised her fork after spearing a big bite of her breakfast. She stopped just short of reaching her mouth when a high-pitched voice carried across the small diner. "Callie Lang! Oh my gosh! I haven't seen you in so long! How are you?"

Sliding the bite off her fork into her mouth, Kat zeroed in on the petite woman who practically accosted a slender blonde walking from the direction of the ladies' room. The woman called Callie flashed a friendly smile at the loud woman as they embraced, but Kat suspected from Callie's expression that she failed to recognize the other woman.

"I'm fine. How are you?" Callie pulled away from the embrace.

"Doing well. Thank you for asking. Your sister tells me you landed a nice new job, and I must say being a working woman agrees with you. Are you enjoying it?"

Callie nodded. "Yes. I'm the office manager for a brand-new security firm. We're still in the process of interviewing and hiring the staff and building our client base, so we've been busy. I was just about to head to work early. Our computer analyst resigned unexpectedly yesterday, and we're interviewing new prospects all day. I'd better get going. It was good to see you."

Kat unabashedly listened. A security firm. Hiring a computer analyst. She almost couldn't believe she'd heard correctly. She was more experienced as a computer programmer, but her skills could be suited for an analyst position. Here she was eating her last dollar, wondering how she was going to be able to keep living in her car with cooler weather approaching. Then she overhears about a job in her field in the town she'd fallen in love with on the very morning she was set to move on. Lady Luck was *finally* giving her a break.

She looked back just as Callie Lang exited with her purse slung over her shoulder. She held a drink carrier full of coffees and a brown paper bag. Kat dropped her eyes to her barely eaten stack of pancakes before making up her mind. Hastily shoving another bite of her breakfast into her mouth, she slapped her money on the table, slipped out of the booth and ran to the door before Callie could disappear.

The diner sat in the middle of Grayson Cove, a draw for locals and tourists alike. The sun shone just enough to take the bite out of the air. Traffic moved steadily through town, but Callie Lang didn't step into a car. She kept up a hurried pace down the sidewalk.

Kat set off after the other woman, hoping she wouldn't notice she was being followed. After a couple of blocks with some turns thrown in, Callie walked through a set of double doors belonging to a two-story brick building. The office building was situated between a boutique and a law office and seemed out of place among the small store fronts along the street.

Taking a deep breath and keeping a leisurely pace, Kat walked past the building, casting a quick glance through the windows. Seeing no one inside, she returned to peering more closely through the pane. There was no sign on the building or the doors, but as she focused on the inside of the lobby, she read the metal letters affixed to the back wall behind a large reception desk. *Knight Security and Investigations.*

Her mouth curved in a wide smile. This was it. This would be the game changer, the place where she would turn her life around. She would make sure of it. The firm wasn't open to the public yet, but probably would be soon, she guessed, based on what she'd overheard. She had little time to clean up, find something suitable to wear, and return before they could give the job to someone else.

No way was she letting that happen.

§

Tristin Knight bit into the doughnut as if his life depended on it. And considering the busy day ahead of him, it probably did.

His administrative assistant came to work prepared, bringing coffees and sugary pastries to start the day. The diner a few blocks over had some of the best baked goods he'd ever tasted, but something about a simple glazed doughnut never failed to tempt him. Add to it a good cup of coffee, and he was ready to face a long morning of job interviews.

When Tristin took a leap of faith to start his own company, Knight Security and Investigations, he never imagined the hardest part would be finding the right employees to carry out his vision. He imagined a company consisting of two sides – one that handled private security and private investigations cases, and the other that would be much more. He thought building a reputation and finding clients would be the biggest challenge.

He had been wrong.

Getting the right staff in place was critical to attracting clients, and so far, the task proved more difficult than he expected. The computer analyst would be key to the special ops side of the business, and Tristin thought he'd struck gold with his first techie. The guy was smart, always speaking computer jargon that went over everyone's head. The tech's first task was to equip the command center, as Tristin dubbed the largest space in the building. He envisioned the command center to be a base of operation for KSI's cases. Other than ordering an expensive load of equipment, the tech had been useless. The guy eventually quit, saying he didn't want to work in a "hostile work environment."

Tristin had laughed. He couldn't help himself. He knew the techie was intimidated by the soldiers he'd employed so far – all three of them. The guys had the special skills he was looking for, and at the same time, they were well suited to the private security and investigations side of the business – the official "face" of Knight Security and Investigations. But their training would be the backbone of the other side of the company, the one only a select few would be aware of. Their missions would be classified and often dangerous, the sort of ops the government or law enforcement agencies couldn't handle alone.

His former commanding officer had given him the idea after he and most of his Navy SEAL team had been injured on a mission gone wrong. Instead of taking out insurgents, his team had walked into an ambush that left his team in need of aid. His own injury prompted a medical discharge, and he battled bitterness and depression at seeing his military career disappear before his eyes.

At the time, his CO had shown up on his doorstep, an expensive bottle of Scotch in his hand. As the two proceeded to empty the bottle and shoot the shit, his CO had told him about all the missions which went unfulfilled for various reasons and how his decision to hire a group of mercenaries to handle a particular mission haunted him. Mercenaries were known for their shoot-first-ask-questions-later attitude while soldiers were trained to access and respond to achieve the best possible outcome.

His CO's story stuck with him until he'd taken the finances he'd accumulated over the years and poured them into his new business. He hired Callie first to help him get organized. Then he called on another recently retired SEAL, Jayson Colter, to come on board. Jayson, or Jay as everyone called him, and his team had worked with Tristin's team on the mission that had gotten them sent home. Jay's team had pulled the others out of the line of fire, getting them out alive. The mission had been Jay's last before his retirement. Tristin couldn't think of another solider he'd rather have at his side as he assembled what he'd already dubbed the Alpha Team.

Former Marine Jordan Raines accepted the job as security guard for the office. The last thing he wanted was for the cases his company worked to put a target on his employees. He couldn't sell the security work of his company and ignore its own security needs.

Then there was Mason "Brick" Coffey, also a Marine, who was more than happy to take the lead on the private investigation and security services the company provided. With Callie running the office, all he needed was a tech.

Hopefully, he would remedy that today, as Callie reminded him when she breezed into his office earlier.

"You have fourteen coming in for interviews today. Most are recent graduates the local colleges and universities referred to us, some are coming from the employment agency I contacted, and others responded to the online ad we placed with a job search website."

"Was there no way to narrow the list down before we started the interview process?" Tristin was already tired of this part, but unfortunately there wasn't anyone he could delegate the responsibility to.

"There wasn't time." Callie sat on one of the heavy oak chairs. "Justin resigned yesterday, and you said you wanted to hire his replacement ASAP. They all meet the qualifications. I'll collect their resumes as they arrive, and you can review them before you speak with them. Here's the first one."

Tristin nodded, not bothering to look at the paper she placed on his desk. "I need one more doughnut before we get started."

Callie smiled. "That's fine. His interview wasn't scheduled to begin for another five minutes or so. Oh, and your brother is here. He said he wanted to finish setting up the equipment for you before he headed in to work."

Tristin grunted. His twin brother, Travis, had the exact skills he was looking for in a computer analyst, and he'd been filling in when needed until Tristin could hire the right person. Since he already had a reliable staff in place, Travis was able to spend a few hours each day until he was needed at the fitness center he owned.

"Too bad Travis is busy with his own business, or the job search would be over."

Callie rose from her seat across from Tristin's desk. "He said he would pop in before he left. Buzz me when you're ready to start the interviews."

Tristin nodded but was already reaching for another glazed doughnut. Callie left just as Jay Colter filled the doorway with his considerable frame. He lightly tapped on the open office door. Tristin motioned for him to come in before polishing off his doughnut.

"Good news, Tryst." Jay never bothered with such formalities as saying good morning or calling him boss or Mr. Knight. His use of Tristin's nickname – given to him as an ode to his womanizing ways – spoke of the friendship the two SEALS shared almost from the moment they met. "Sam Montgomery's on board."

"That's great! 'Bout damn time something good happened around here," Tristin drawled.

Sam possessed quite a reputation as an Army Ranger before working a stint for the FBI. The seasoned veteran was the right addition to the Alpha Team, and Jay had been pulling no punches in convincing the Ranger to sign on.

"He's coming in later today to talk salary and sign the employment paperwork. Hopefully you'll have a new computer geek hired to start the required background check," Jay replied with a teasing grin.

"Why can't your FBI buddy give us a referral there too? Then I could cancel all of the interviews and start trying to line up paying customers."

Jay slid his hands into his jean pockets. "Sorry. The FBI already employs the best hackers in the business. I doubt anything we could offer would entice them to make a career move."

"Don't remind me," Tristin grumbled, not wanting to dwell on how quickly the company's finances would dwindle if clients didn't start rolling in. "Want to help me with the interviews?"

"Nope," Jay said, already walking to the door. "I'm meeting with who I hope will be our next Alpha Team member. Griffin Tyler. He's a former fighter pilot. He's a cocky SOB, but he's smart. His record is solid. I'll keep you posted."

The team leader closed the office door behind him as he left. Tristin exhaled before taking a long swig of his coffee. He pushed up from his desk. The sooner he started the interviews, the sooner he could find a new tech. Then he could blow off steam with a beer at his favorite bar, Torch. He might even find a lovely woman to take the edge off his stress.

Chapter Two

Kat did her best to school her features, so her nerves didn't show. She had to be prepared to talk herself into an interview. Yet the moment she laid eyes on the burly security guard manning the lobby of Knight Security and Investigations, her false bravado shook. Her hands smoothed the faint wrinkles in her suit as her heels clicked against the tile floor. The walk to the receptionist desk seemed too long, and she pasted a smile on her face, hoping the guard wouldn't guess she was moments away from bolting.

"May I help you?" His tone was friendly, but his face was unreadable. Hair buzzed close to his scalp, faint lines creased the skin around his eyes and mouth. His frame was tall, bulky and imposing, but his dark eyes softened as she stopped in front of the desk.

"I'm here for the interview." She was relieved to hear her voice sound steady even though her nerves sang with tension.

"This way."

He moved to the elevator and scanned the badge attached to the pocket of his uniform by a retractable clip. "Go to the second floor and check in with Callie. You'll see her at the desk when you step off the elevator. Good luck." And he smiled, a wide, friendly gesture that transformed his face from intimidating to warm and welcoming.

Kat returned the smile without thought. "Thank you."

The short elevator ride allowed her to take a couple of deep, calming breaths. When the doors opened, she stepped into the small waiting room. The woman she already knew as Callie occupied a desk but spoke on the phone instead of acknowledging Kat's presence. Her shoes clicked against the floor as she took only a couple of steps, and Callie jerked her head around to pierce her with a harsh stare, as if her footsteps were purposely too loud. She wasn't sure why, but she mouthed a quick "I'm sorry" before occupying the closest empty chair.

Her eyes rested on a man also seated in the waiting area. His suit was impeccably tailored, his eyes glued to the smart phone in his hand. He never acknowledged her, not that she really expected him too. But studying him brought to the surface her doubts about how she looked.

After finding the building that morning, she'd run back to her car to head to a service station. She had made quick work of getting ready in the station's restroom and returned to the firm shortly after it opened at nine.

The only hiccup was finding the service station's bathroom occupied when she arrived. After she'd waited for ten minutes, a rather large woman exited, leaving a waft of smelly air behind her. Kat gagged more times than she wanted to think about as she'd washed up and donned her suit. She was hesitant to spend time washing, drying and styling her hair, so she used dry shampoo to freshen her locks, pulling a few strands away from her face and securing them in a barrette. Her makeup was subtle, highlighting the slight slant to her dark eyes, her thick lashes, and her high cheekbones.

Callie hung up the phone and stood. "May I help you with something?"

Kat approached her desk with a big smile. "I'm here for an interview. For the computer analyst position."

"You don't have an appointment."

Kat blinked at the cool tone. "What? How do you even know that? You didn't ask my name."

"Because I have a list of the people we're interviewing today, and the first two appointments are gentlemen. I'm sorry, but you must have an appointment to be interviewed. And we are booked up today."

The phone rang against, and Callie bade her a quick farewell before answering. Kat turned and realized she had gained the attention of the other man in the waiting room. His look was sympathetic, but then he returned to his phone, effectively dismissing her as well.

Kat hated the dejected feeling weighing in her chest. All she needed was a chance. She didn't have to know the job duties to know she could do the job well. But if the owner talked to one of the other analyst wannabes first, she could kiss this opportunity goodbye. She wasn't about to let that happen.

Kat looked over her shoulder at Callie, who was writing on a notepad as she spoke into the phone. She moved closer to the elevator to gain a better view of the hallway to her right. Doors lined the hallway on either side, but she guessed the one at the end in the corner of the building housed the person she needed to see.

A man passed the doorway to the lobby heading down the hall in the direction where she looked. Dressed in jeans and a T-shirt, he stood several inches taller than her, his body lean and muscular. His skin was deeply tanned, making his thick hair appear shockingly blond. He was hot enough to put Kat's libido in a twist under different circumstances. He didn't fit the image of a corporate CEO, but when he stepped without hesitation through the door to the office she'd been eyeing, Kat knew that was exactly who he was.

With Callie distracted, Kat knew the time was now to make her move. She power-walked from the lobby down the hallway, almost running to the corner office. Hearing a loud "hey" from behind her, she realized her retreat had been noticed. She didn't have a lot of time, so she frantically pushed through the office door.

She all but stumbled inside, drawing up short as her gaze landed on not one but two men. They stood eye-to-eye, their blond hair, square jaws and broad shoulders mirror images of each other. Kat's mouth fell open as she looked from one man to the other.

"There are two of you!" Her palm jerked up to slap her mouth closed, and her eyes shut in mortification.

She'd just screwed up the first impression she was counting on to land her the job she was desperate to get.

§

Tristin's efforts to start his workday were interrupted by his brother sailing through his office door without bothering with a knock. Travis was dressed more for a day at his job than a day at KSI, and Tristin decided against teasing him about that fact. As much as he would love his twin to join him in building his company, Travis was successful operating his own business, Knight and Day Fitness Center.

Growing up, the brothers were inseparable, but as they grew older, they chose different paths for their lives. Tristin enlisted in the military while Travis opted for the police academy, eventually rising to the ranks of detective and developing his skills as a computer programmer. Tristin was still serving with the SEALS when Travis decided to shift careers for something he could call his own.

As lucrative as the fitness center was, Tristin couldn't stop wishing his brother would come on board at KSI. The two Knight brothers joining forces to set the world on fire was a tempting dream. Unfortunately, he settled for having Travis fill in when Tristin needed him.

"You're just in time to help me interview computer geeks to take Justin's place." Tristin greeted his brother with his most charming smile.

"Don't think so, baby brother."

Tristin scowled at his brother, who grinned in response. Travis enjoyed rubbing in the fact he was born a whole two minutes before his twin.

"I've got my own work to do. But I have your equipment set up. Justin spared no expense, and you've got a high-quality command center in place. You just need someone to operate it."

"No kidding," Tristin groaned.

"It'll work out. I told Callie to call me if I need to vet anyone you want to hire."

"Thanks for your help, man. Meet up at Torch later?" Tristin was already looking forward to grabbing a beer at their favorite bar and grill later.

"Can't. Got a date. And now I have to get to work. Later, Tryst."

Before Travis could leave, the door flew open. A woman Tristin had never seen before stumbled in. She stood in front of the two brothers slightly out of breath. Tristin barely noticed how her head swiveled as she studied the brothers. As if something struck him dumb, he stood rooted to the floor, his body aflame as he committed everything about this woman to memory.

She stood just a few inches shorter than his six-foot-one frame. Her suit jacket and slacks fit her willowy frame well. Her dark hair was pulled away from her face, the ebony tendrils falling down her back. Flawless olive skin complemented her full pink lips and wide eyes. Those eyes held Tristin captive. They slanted slightly at the corners, their dark pools fathomless even as they registered her surprise. They were fringed with thick, inky lashes.

"There are two of you."

Her stating the obvious was not an uncommon occurrence for the brothers. They'd heard it more than once when people met them without first knowing they were twins. It ranked right up there with "you look just alike" and "you must be twins."

The woman covered her mouth as if she never meant for the words to pass her lips, and she closed those amazing eyes. Tristin had never seen anything so adorable. He almost begged her to open her eyes, already missing their dark beauty.

"There are, but not for long," Travis spoke up. "I was just leaving. I'm guessing you're here to talk to the boss."

Callie followed close on the woman's heels, giving her a glare before addressing her boss. "I'm sorry, Tristin. She ran past me before I could stop her. Want me to call Jay or Jordan to escort her out?"

"No." Tristin wasn't usually this blunt, but his mind couldn't think of anything else to say, but he knew without a doubt he did not want this woman to leave.

"All right," Callie said reluctantly, eyeing her boss curiously. "Just let me know if you change your mind."

The door closed behind his assistant, and the stranger dropped her hand as she opened her eyes. Tristin saw the sudden burst of confidence infusing into her expression and her stance.

"Um, sorry about that. I just didn't want to miss an opportunity to talk with you. I'm here for the computer analyst job. I know you have a day full of interviews, and I technically don't have an appointment, but I'm definitely the one you want to hire. I'm the perfect person for the job. It would be a mistake to talk to anyone else."

Her voice washed over Tristin, warming his blood. She spoke clearly with a gentle huskiness he'd never heard in a woman's voice before. His imagination transported him to his bedroom, with her lying naked on his sheets, her dark hair spread across his pillow. And she whispered with her sexy voice directly into his ear, describing all the naughty things she wanted him to do to her.

Tristin felt his brother regarding him curiously since he had not yet spoken to the woman barging into his office. He wasn't sure he could escape the sexual haze fogging his senses.

"Well," Travis continued when his brother failed to make a sound. "That's a bold claim to make."

"I can back it up," she quickly said. "I was recruited while I was in college to work for Bingham Technologies as part of their programming team. Since they were a small company, I've done everything from computer programming to web development to cyber security."

"Bingham Technologies? I've read about them. They're a top-rate company, but I heard they had some financial difficulties," Travis said.

She pursed her lips, and Tristin fought the overwhelming urge to kiss that full mouth.

"Yes, that's true. To be completely honest with you, I was laid off from the company when they decided to close due to their financial troubles. But it doesn't change the fact my skill set makes me the ideal person for this job," she insisted.

"What's your name?" Tristin finally spoke. He could care less about her qualifications for the job, but he burned to know more about her – what she liked, what she hated, what she was passionate about. But he would start with her name.

"Oh, I guess I should have told you already. I'm Katarina Walsh."

"Katarina," he repeated, savoring the feel of her name on his lips.

She cleared her throat. "Actually, most people call me Kat. Katarina is such a mouthful to say."

Her name was beautiful and suited her. He wanted to tell her, but his mind wouldn't communicate with his tongue to voice the words. Again, Travis came to his rescue.

"Well, Miss Walsh, my brother has a lot of people to interview today. Why don't you just leave your resume with Callie at the front desk, and they'll be in touch."

"I can do that, but I don't need one to tell you what you'll figure out after interviewing just one of the people on your schedule today. I'm different from all of them. Do you know what your first candidate is doing right now? He is on his phone. Do you know what that means? He has a life and outside interests to distract him from his work. I have no such issue. I'm new to town, and I can promise you I will live, eat and breathe this job. I know that's what you need being a new company. I promise you, Mr. Knight, you will not regret taking a chance on me."

Her dark eyes flashed with the same fervor lacing her words. Her cheeks flushed becomingly from her passionate speech. Travis opened his mouth, but this time, Tristin beat him to the punch.

"The job is yours. When can you start?"

Chapter Three

Tristin watched Jay pace the length of his office while Travis and Callie occupied the two chairs opposite his desk. They assembled in his office fifteen minutes ago in what he could only call an intervention. He understood their concern. Thinking back now, he stunned himself with his knee-jerk reaction to Katarina Walsh. He didn't make snap decisions, especially when it came to his fledgling business.

"She is a college dropout, and you've entrusted her to handle the entire set-up of the command center. How do you know she's going to be able to handle the stresses of the job?" Callie questioned in her ever-practical way.

"She's a kid. And you're expecting the Alpha Team to put their lives in the hands of a kid just because you want to nail her," Jay picked up the diatribe Tristin had been listening to since the trio barged into his office.

"Stop!" Tristin finally responded. "I didn't hire her because I want to nail her. If she's my employee, that can't happen. Give it a rest already."

"I was in the room when you met her, remember?" Travis countered. "All the blood left your head and went straight to your groin. I get it, man. She's gorgeous, but this is your business we're talking about. You can't screw around."

Tristin couldn't deny his reaction to her. He'd been instantly attracted to women before, but he'd never responded to a woman the way he did to Katarina. Something about her intrigued him, but hiring her had nothing to do with the fact she was the most beautiful and sexy woman he'd ever laid eyes on. Though he wanted to know more about her and be near her, he had given her the job for one reason and one reason only – his gut. She stood in his office giving him all the reasons why he should hire her without talking with anyone else. When she spoke of the passion and dedication she'd give to the job, his gut believed her. He trusted his gut, plain and simple. He wasn't about to deny it now, and he wasn't about to justify his actions to anyone.

He was the boss, dammit.

"Travis, you admitted her resume was impressive, and her references confirmed she had the skills – and then some – to do the job. Callie, you said we needed to find someone with the backbone to provide technical support in the life and death situations we'll be dealing with. Well, if having the balls to sneak past you into my office and proceed to convince me why she's different from the rest isn't having backbone, then I don't know what else you'd call it. And Jay, have you even met Kat? Have you talked to her, or are you just listening to the crap these two are feeding you?

"The bottom line is this is my company, she's my hire, and you all should respect my decision. If this backfires on me, then it backfires on me. I know you all have more important things to do besides being here in my office reading me the riot act."

Finally releasing his frustration, Tristin felt damn good. He rose from his desk and crossed to the door.

"Where are you going?" Jay demanded.

"None of your business." Tristin slammed the door behind him.

He hesitated. He wanted to seek out Katarina more than he wanted to take his next breath. But spending any unnecessary time with her would only add fuel to the fires of doubt brewing in his staff. Instead, he left the building altogether. Stepping into his black SUV, he sped out of the parking lot with no destination in mind.

§

Kat had stepped into computer hacker heaven.

She had been prepared to do whatever she needed to get the job, but other than a quick sale of her skills, nothing else was needed. The owner, Tristin Knight, seemed to be a man of few words, but he'd obviously seen her potential to hire her on the spot. His brother, however, never stopped talking. She read his disapproval of his brother's hiring her in his expression and the tenseness of his shoulders. Kat didn't care. She had a job, and she would make the most of it for as long as it lasted.

The receptionist had shown her to the command center, which exceeded her expectations. The workspace was too large for just her, but she was grateful to be solo for the moment. The equipment was state-of-the-art with all the tools she could ever want. Callie told her to get settled and familiarize herself with the equipment. Since she had only needed thirty minutes to do that and she had no other instructions on what she was supposed to be doing, Kat decided to take initiative.

Kat never liked to sit idle. Easily bored, she learned to keep herself busy, especially if she had access to a computer. She figured out the login to the system and began poking around the KSI network. The security was adequate, but the company was supposed to provide private security and PI services, if the company name was any indication. They would be privy to client's private information, so Kat believed the security could be better.

She easily lost herself in her work, feeling an escape from the worry and stress weighing on her since she lost her job. She found comfort in the ones and zeros. The more complex the code, the more she thrived on the challenge.

Her concentration broke when she heard the gentle swoosh of the command center door opening and closing.

“Let me finish this line of code before I lose my train of thought,” she said without slowing her keystrokes.

“I’m surprised you knew I was here. You seemed pretty intent on whatever it is you’re doing.”

The deep voice wasn’t one she’d heard before, and she had no idea who just stepped into the command center. She sensed him moving closer to her, thanks to the hyper sense of awareness she developed from living in her car. She wasn’t sure what he expected her to say, but she couldn’t stop herself from filling the silence anyway.

“I would think you guys would be glad I’m so intense. I just beefed up your cybersecurity. Any hacker would lose his mind trying to breech this system.”

“How do we know you aren’t the one breeching the system?” She could feel the man standing over her, but she was determined not to show how he rattled her.

“You don’t. And since you don’t know for sure, it probably wasn’t very smart to leave me in here by myself for the last—” She glanced at the clock in the corner of her monitor. “—two hours.”

He chuckled, stopping where she could study him out of her peripheral. Tall, massive build, dark hair to match the dark beard obscuring his face, his confidence and swagger spoke of someone who showed no fear.

“You have me at a disadvantage since you know who I am, but I have no idea who you are. Do you even work here?”

“I do,” he drawled. “I’m Jay.”

She glanced up at him briefly. With a sigh, she inputted the last line of code before pushing the desk chair back from the computer. She crossed her arms over her chest as she regarded him.

“Look. Tell your boss if he’s regretting his decision to hire me, then he can come in here and fire me himself. He doesn’t have to send his goon squad.”

Jay quirked a brow. "Goon squad? Wow. That's a new one. No one's ever called me a goon."

"That you know of," she mumbled, but she kept her tone loud enough for him to hear.

He smirked. "Tell me something, Katarina. Why did you want this job bad enough to barge your way into Tryst's office this morning?"

"Tryst?" This time, she was the one raising a questioning brow.

"Tristin. Tristin Knight. The guy who owns this place."

"Must be nice to be on a semi-first name basis with the boss," she teased, hoping to lighten up the guy's intense stare.

"We worked together as Navy SEALs some time ago, so he's a friend as well as my boss. Are you going to answer my question?"

"Jay, you know from reading my resume I'm been out of work for months now. I haven't had the best of luck in finding work, and I wasn't expecting to find anything in this town either. I was set to move on when I heard about this job," she explained.

"You *heard* about the job?" he countered.

"Yes, I overheard Callie telling someone at the diner this morning about interviewing computer analysts. I followed her here, so I'd know what company was doing the interviews. Then I showed up when you opened this morning. Anything else you'd like to know? My blood type? My favorite ice cream? The name of my childhood pet?"

"Kind of defensive, aren't you?"

Kat rolled her eyes. "Wouldn't you be if people were questioning your motives? I'm not exactly sure what the rest of you have against me, but that's your problem. If it's an issue for the boss, then he can fire me himself. In the meantime, I'm going to do my job. Well, at least what I think my job is. No one has told me yet what my responsibilities are."

"Why upgrade the network security if no one told you to?" Jay demanded.

"Because it should be the first thing you had your new computer analyst do. I'm guessing you want your client and employee files to be as secure as possible, and while the security you had in place was adequate, it could always be stronger. Your client information gets stolen, and your business is sunk. Period."

Jay grew quiet, but his intense stare never let up. She fought the urge to shift in her seat. She refused to let this man intimidate her. Her livelihood depended on not failing now.

After several minutes passed, he finally lifted his chin to her. A sign of respect, maybe? She released the breath she'd been holding.

"We're pretty close knit around here. Tristin has invested a lot into starting this company. You can't blame us for wanting to watch out for his best interests," Jay eventually told her.

"I'm not out to bring his company down in any way. I just need a paycheck. That's all."

"I'll let you get back to work then." He held her gaze for a long moment and then moved to the door.

"Jay." He paused and turned. "Who is supposed to tell me what I need to be doing?"

"I'm guessing once Tristin and Travis make up, the boss will have Travis work with you. He's the only resident computer techie we have around here."

"Travis works here too?" she asked in surprise.

"No, he's just helping. See you around, Katarina."

"Call me Kat," she called after his retreating form. Jay didn't reply, but Kat was sure he heard her.

Though she was grateful to be alone again, she didn't go back to her work right away. Her mind mulled over Jay's words. *Once Tristin and Travis make up*. Were they fighting because of her? All she had on her mind was doing whatever it took to get the job. Causing a rift between the brothers was never her intent.

Her own relationship with her brother, Nick, had always been strained. Fourteen years her senior, Nick treated her more as a child than a sibling. They couldn't be more different. He was always rigid, a stickler for rules, and always concerned with what others' thought of him. Growing up, he made his decisions based on what would earn him praise with their parents. As an adult, his life revolved around how successful he could be with his career and how revered he could be in society.

While Nick deemed success to be based on his bank account and social status, Kat had other ideas. Though she found a career using her talents, she never made her choices based on money or status. When Bingham Technologies recruited her during her senior year of college, she knew the job would give hands-on experience unlike what she would receive in school. The job was all she could dream of, so when the company informed her she was being laid off due to financial difficulties, she'd believed her skills would land her a new job as easily as she found the first one.

Then came the phone call from Nick.

"You need to come home. It's Mom. She's not well, Kat, and we need to make some decisions."

Nick's version of "not well" consisted of a diagnosis of early onset Alzheimer's disease. The demands of her job left her with little time to visit home, but she knew from her phone conversations that her mother was becoming forgetful. Her mother explained it away with the aging process, but Nick's call told her Lori's condition went beyond old age.

Kat moved back home and found an IT job that was well below her advanced skill sets, but she had the flexibility to help with her mother's care. Lori's decline seemed to happen quickly, and Kat lost her job because of the many times she had to miss work to care for her mother. Nick convinced her the time had come to sell their childhood home to pay for long-term care for their mother. Kat was left without a job and a home and was forced to stay with Nick and his wife Brenda.

Kat shuddered as she remembered the stressful time with her brother. He never missed a moment to remind her she needed to pull her weight in paying for their mother's care. Then he would follow that up with his judgment about what he deemed her immature life choices. She grew to hate her life and to resent the circumstances that left her dependent on a brother who didn't respect her.

So, she hit the road. Determined to still be close enough to visit her mother, she moved from town to city in search of a job and a new home. She put much-needed distance between her and Nick, though he managed to administer his regular dose of disapproval via phone calls.

Her eyes rested on the computer as she thought of how her relationship with Nick was fractured beyond repair. Instead of supporting each other through a difficult time, they couldn't stand to be near each other.

And now she was the cause of a rift between Tristin and his brother, something she would never want to do. Family was too important, and this job couldn't take precedence over that. As much as she didn't want to make the decision, she knew it was the right thing to do.

She could complete her work for today, and then she would move on as planned. The day's wages would be enough to get her to the next town, where she'd already identified a couple of job leads. Then Tristin Knight could get back on track with his brother and his employees.

Kat went back to work. Her plan made sense, even if her keen disappointment made no sense at all.

Chapter Four

Tristin waited until well after his employees left for the day before he returned to KSI. He left Callie to cancel all the computer analyst interviews. He left Jay to do his own thing, only responding to a text to say he was fine, but he would not be back today. He left Travis to go to his own job, never receiving any kind of communication from him. No more heated words, no apology, nothing.

After a couple of hours, once he'd cooled down, he came to the realization they all had a point. His gut told him to give Kat a chance, but his hormones had him uttering the words, "The job is yours." He knew if he didn't give her a job, she would walk out of his office, and he'd never see her again. He wasn't sure why he cared, and he sure as hell didn't want to analyze how Kat had gotten under his skin so fast. But he would have to deal with the consequences of his knee-jerk decision.

Some corporate CEO he was.

His day had not been a total loss. He contacted a military colleague of his who gave him a lead of a possible member for the Alpha Team. Zane Wilder was known as a loner who had a tendency to go rogue, but his skills as an Army sharpshooter were second to none. Tristin wanted to check him out more before giving his name to Jay. Something told him the sharpshooter and the team leader would clash more than they got along, but Tristin believed their differences could only make the team stronger. Jay may fight him on this, but he'd be ready to defend his decision.

If only he could say the same for his choice to hire Katarina Walsh.

When he made it back to KSI, he was surprised to find Jordan still manning his post. The security guard typically cleared out once the employees left for the day, making his presence at this late hour puzzling.

"Hey, boss. Everybody's been wondering where you went off to." Jordan's lighthearted tone eased Tristin's anxieties.

"Why are you still here, man? You should get home to the wife before she thinks I'm holding you hostage."

"Yeah, I didn't feel right leaving her here by herself. I called Stella to tell her I'd be late getting home. I'll make it up to her this weekend." The burly guard wagged his brows suggestively, pulling a guffaw from his boss.

"Callie's here waiting for me, huh?" Tristin shouldn't have been surprised. Callie was invaluable as his assistant. She often stayed late to help him catch up on any pressing business he'd been too busy to handle during regular work hours.

"No, sir, not Callie. She waited around a little while, but she finally cut out about seven or so. The new girl is still here. I took her a key card to get in and out of the building after hours, but I still didn't feel right leaving her here by herself on her first day."

"Kat is here? What is she doing?" Tristin left before having a chance to talk to her about the job. He couldn't imagine what she would be doing at the office this late when no one left her any instructions.

Jordan chuckled. "No clue. I don't understand computer stuff. Jay and Callie checked in on her off and on all day, but no one's really bothered her. She's barely left the command center to do more than take a leak."

Cameras around the building fed into the monitors at Jordan's desk, giving him a direct view of most of the comings and goings of people inside the building. The security measure was not a necessity now, but it would be important once they began the sensitive work he had in mind for the Alpha Team.

"She leave for lunch?" Tristin asked as his gaze fell to the take-out bag in his own hand.

"She hasn't left since she walked in the door this morning. She's working like a woman possessed."

Tristin frowned. He appreciated hard work in his employees, but he didn't like the idea of them working without a break unless the occasion was serious enough to warrant it. He especially didn't like the idea of Kat not taking care of her basic needs, like eating.

"Thanks, Jordan. Go ahead and head home to Stella. I'm going to send our new analyst home as well. It's long past time for you guys to call it a day."

"What about you, Tryst? If you're going to be a while, I don't care to hang around."

"No need. I'll be fine, but thanks for the offer. Enjoy the rest of your night."

Waving goodbye to the guard, Tristin rode the elevator up to the second floor but bypassed his office for the command center. Sure enough, Katarina Walsh sat at the computer, her fingers flying over the keyboard. He studied her as she worked, only the light from the monitors illuminating her lovely face. She paused to tilt her head from side to side, stretching her neck. She placed her hands on the small of her back and leaned back to stretch. Tristin's mouth went dry, imagining her breasts thrusting forward with the move, stretching the fabric of her shirt. She had kicked off her shoes, and the sight of her bare feet fascinated him.

He stepped inside the command center but paused when she jumped in her chair. She spun around to face him as her hand rose to cover her heart. She visibly relaxed when she recognized his silhouette.

"Oh, Mr. Knight, it's you. I didn't think anyone else was here."

He crossed the room, unable to deny his need to be close to her. "I just sent Jordan home, which is where you should be. It's late."

She smiled, and Tristin felt its impact like a punch to the gut. "It's fine. It's really not that—" Her voice trailed off as she noticed the time in the corner of her monitor. "Oh, I didn't realize. I lost track of time. I told Jordan he didn't have to wait for me. He said he could lock up, and I could use my keycard to get out without setting off the security alarm."

Tristin placed the takeout bag on the table next to her computer. "It's fine, Kat. It's his job. He told me you skipped lunch. You must be starving. Eat and then I'll take you home."

"I have my car," she replied absently as she peered inside the bag. "You brought me dinner? How did you know I was still here?"

"Jordan told me you hadn't eaten all day," he said, evading her questions. "You need to eat." Tristin pulled up a computer chair and settled his tired frame onto the squeaky seat.

Kat's eyes narrowed. "I'm not eating your dinner."

He grinned at how easily she figured him out. "I never said it was my dinner."

She crossed her arms over her chest, the maneuver thrusting her full breasts up. Tristin schooled his expression, but heat suffused his body. She shot him a mutinous glare, and his grin widened. Damn, she was cute.

"I'm not eating your dinner."

"Consider it an apology. I left you here to your own devices on your first day. I never meant for you to work after hours or even through your lunch break. Please eat, Katarina. I'll worry about you if you don't."

Her expression softened. She glanced back in the bag before looking to him again. "It's Kat. And thank you, Mr. Knight. But I won't eat unless you join me. I won't feel right eating in front of you when this was supposed to your dinner. There's plenty here, and Chinese food fills me up pretty fast. I couldn't possibly eat it all by myself."

"It's Tristin. And yes, I will eat with you."

Moving to an empty table along the wall behind her, she started pulling out the to-go containers from the bag while Tristin wished she would say his name. He wanted to hear it just once coming from her sexy mouth. When her brow furrowed as she stared into the bag, all he could think about was how adorable she was.

"There's only one fork. Is there a breakroom around here? I can go look for another one," she said absently.

"I can use the chopsticks," he offered.

"You sure? I don't mind going to look," she said even as she handed him the pack of chopsticks.

Without another word, he opened the pack, picked up the closest container, and dug into the orange chicken. As juvenile as it seemed, he wanted her to be impressed with his use of the eating utensil. He wanted to impress her with something because she impressed him quite a bit, and he barely knew her.

She tore open the cellophane packaging around the fork and started winding lo mein noodles around the prongs. Tristin watched her lips close around the fork, her jaw working to chew the food and her throat constricting as she swallowed. Tristin swallowed a groan, and he shifted in his chair to try and ease the sudden discomfort in his pants. *Get a grip, Tryst.* Since when did a woman eating Chinese food like it was her last meal become such a turn on?

"What have you been working on all day?" He hoped shop talk would cool his libido.

"Well," she began around a mouthful of noodles. "I've upgraded your firewalls and enhanced security for your network. What you had before was fine, but I was thinking, with the personal information you might likely collect on your clients, you want to be able to assure them everything is extremely secure. Like government level secure. Then I got to thinking you probably would want your PIs to share updates on their cases with you. Being the CEO, you want to stay up to date on everything, right? So, I built in an encryption system to send secure emails back and forth. Each employee would have a unique decryption code. When they get an encrypted email, they'll be prompted to enter their decryption code before they can open the email."

"Wow. You've been busy."

Kat looked at him sheepishly. She sat down the container of lo mein and reached for an egg roll. "Yeah. I got carried away. Your system is amazing, and it was kind of fun getting to work on it all day."

He could see a love for her work in the way her face lit up and the way her dark eyes sparkled. He didn't understand all the ins and outs of computer programming, but he believed he could listen to Kat talk about it nonstop and never grow tired of hearing her. As long as he could see the happiness on her face as she spoke.

"Sounds like you kept yourself busy." He was too distracted by her beauty to think of anything better to say.

Her skin flushed, and she lowered her eyes. "I did. But, um, that's not all I did."

She looked every bit like the child caught with her hand in the cookie jar. He raised one questioning eyebrow to prompt her to explain.

She sighed dramatically. "Well, I finished all of the cybersecurity stuff by early afternoon. I got bored and started thinking. So, I ended up adding some other features for you, being the CEO and all. If anyone sends an encrypted email to someone outside of KSI, you automatically receive a notification. All the emails will be stored on the network in a password-protected file only you have access to. The password is temporary right now. You'll have to go in and reset it. I figured if someone is sending information outside the company they shouldn't, you need to know about it sooner rather than later. I also noticed the security camera feeds only ran to Jordan's computers. I spliced the feed, and it connects to the computer in your office and the computers here in the command center as well. Just in case."

"And no one told you to do any of this?"

Kat shook her head. "I haven't really spoken to anyone all day. Jordan came in once to check on me, and Callie's walked by a few times. She didn't come in though. Oh, and some guy named Jay came in to make sure I wasn't trying to use you or cheat you or whatever."

Tristin almost choked on his chicken. "*What*? What did Jay say?"

Kat swallowed the last bite of her egg roll and wiped her mouth and hands with a napkin. "It's Okay, Mr. Knight. I understand what's going on. You sort of hired me without really checking me out, and I know everyone is suspicious about why I was fired up to work here. I'm guessing Jay is one of your private investigators, so it's his job to check me out and make sure I'm legit. He's just looking out for you. They all are."

And with that, she erased any doubt he had about hiring her.

Soon. If Kat continued to work here, he would have to tell her more about Jay and his role in the company. He didn't think now was the time, but he knew he would have to have the conversation with her soon.

"You should never have been caught in the middle. I hired you, and if they disagree with the decision, they should take it up with me, not take it out on you. Obviously, you know what you're doing. They'll figure out I made the right call hiring you."

"Why did you? Hire me?"

She surprised herself by asking him what had been lingering in the back of her mind. He could see it by the way her incredible eyes widened. Enclosed in the command center, the only two people in the building, the faint light from the computer monitors created an intimate setting that messed with his senses. If Kat asked him to share his darkest secrets, he didn't think he could deny her.

"Because it was the only way I could think of to keep you from leaving."

She tensed. "I don't understand."

Tristin laughed derisively. "Neither do I. Believe me, I've spent all day trying to figure that out."

Chapter Five

Holy crap!

Kat studied her new boss as if seeing him for the first time. His boyish face sported a square jaw, aquiline nose and high cheekbones any woman would kill for. The lines around his eyes and mouth spoke to how easily he smiled. His wheat-colored hair was clipped short in a disheveled style, adding to his sex appeal. His cerulean eyes shone against his tanned skin, piercing her with their brilliance. His lips were firm and oh, so kissable.

She was on dangerous ground. The men of her past typically fell into two categories – men she dated to have a night out and a free meal and lovers who scratched an itch for her. Neither category carried the possibility of a serious relationship, which is how she liked it. Tristin, on the other hand, did not fall into any of her preconceived categories. Indulging in anything with him outside of a professional relationship was asking for trouble.

"Mr. Knight, I—"

He rose from his chair in one fluid motion. With his hands on the armrests by her side, he pinned her to her seat before she could take a breath.

"I told you to call me Tristin. Say my name, Katarina," he ordered, his face mere inches from hers.

She swallowed the lump suddenly clogging her throat. "Tristin." The word sounded breathy, unlike her usual tone.

Tristin groaned. He moved in until his lips hovered over hers. "I've waited all day to hear you say that."

Kat opened her mouth to respond, and his lips swooped to capture hers. Their tongues tangled with each other in a seductive dance. Desire swirled within her, clouding her mind to everything but the exquisite feel of his lips on hers. His hand rose to cradle the back of her head, tilting it so he could deepen the kiss. He continued his assault until Kat was sure her body would erupt in flames. She reached up to grasp the front of his shirt, grounding herself in his solidness.

He pulled away only the slightest distance. "Katarina," he drawled, and her nipples hardened in response. He said her name reverently as if uttering a romantic endearment.

"Tristin, I—"

He didn't let her finish. He pulled her from her chair, encircling her in his arms. Then he kissed her again, devouring her mouth as a thirsty man desperate for a drop of water. Kat felt her legs give out beneath her, but his firm embrace held her tightly against him. He was all rock-hard muscle. She felt a distinctive ache at the apex between her legs.

He swallowed the moan escaping her throat. He glided his hand around her torso and up her ribs to cup her breast over her shirt. As he kneaded the sensitive mound, she whimpered with the need ripping through her. He released her lips to trail hot kisses along her jaw and down her neck.

"Tristin!"

He smiled against her skin. He raised his head to stare into her eyes. Passion darkened his irises.

"I won't ever get tired of hearing you say my name. God, you're beautiful!"

Kat felt a flutter in her chest. When was the last time someone spoke to her this way, looked at her this way – hell, kissed her this way? She wanted to give into the moment, to lose herself in the passion burning between them. Job be damned. She wanted to touch him and kiss him and spend the night memorizing every inch of his hot body.

She drew a shaky breath and bit back a groan as Tristin's woodsy scent assailed her senses.

"Come with me, Kat. Back to my place. Or yours. I'm not picky." His panty-melting smile was meant to obliterate the last of her defenses.

But his innocent reference to "her place" brought reality crashing back. Her place was her car, which contained every possession she owned. Instead of spending the night with Tristin, she was supposed to be asking for a day's pay and moving on to find work in another town. She pushed against him, the confusion on his face wrenching her heart. He released her, and she stepped away from him until her desk chair bumped the back of her legs. She wrapped her arms around her middle as if to shield herself from the aftermath of what she was about to do.

"I can't stay," she blurted.

He studied her intently. "OK. It's fine, Kat. I would never push you to do something you didn't want to do. It's too soon. I get it."

She shook her head. "No, you don't. Tristin – Mr. Knight, I can't stay. Here. In this job. I have to go."

His eyes narrowed. "What are you talking about? You're leaving because of what just happened?"

"No, I already made up my mind before you came in here. I never wanted to cause any conflict for you, not when you were kind enough to take a chance on me. I think it's better if I move on, and you can find someone for this job who fits in with everyone. What I've made working today is enough to help me get started somewhere else."

"Liar. You don't want to leave. I know you don't." He never

raised his voice, instead addressing her like he was asking about the weather. But his words doused her like a bucket of ice water.

"How can you say that?" she exclaimed. "You don't know me. You know nothing about me."

He moved into her personal space. He didn't touch her. He didn't have to for her body to burn with the electricity surging between them.

"I know you've gotten under my skin. I know I want you in my arms and in my bed more than I've wanted any woman in my life. I know you have lost your mind if you think for one second I'm letting you walk away from the job and from me. It's not happening, Kat."

She wanted to be angry at his highhandedness. She never let a man make demands of her. She was her own person with her own mind. But she couldn't deny she wanted to accept everything he said. She couldn't ignore the fact she wanted him just as much. He was refusing to let her walk away, and she realized leaving was the last thing she wanted to do.

"Do not worry about the people here, Kat. I don't regret my decision to hire you, and eventually they'll realize you're the right choice for this job. If they don't, it doesn't change anything. You belong here."

"If I stay, nothing can happen between us," she said softly, knowing the words were true even as her heart rebelled against them. "You're my boss, and I need this job too much to do anything to mess it up."

He opened his mouth to say something but must have decided against it. He stepped back, his hands finding their way into his pants pocket. His gaze ensnared her, but his expression relaxed. He flashed his signature charming smile.

"The job is yours, Kat, for as long as you want it. I appreciate the hard work you've put in today, but make no mistake. I won't put up with you locking yourself away in here without a break or a meal again. Understood?"

She nodded. "Understood. Thank you, Mr. Knight."

He held up a hand, palm out. "I'm only going to say this once more. The name's Tristin or Tryst. Call me Mr. Knight again, and I'll kiss you until you forget my name altogether."

Kat gasped. She was torn between obeying his command and wanting to kiss him more than she wanted her next breath. She exhaled slowly. *Get a grip, Kat.*

"Tryst?" She tried to keep her tone light and teasing, but she wasn't sure she pulled it off.

He groaned, the sound shooting straight to her girly parts. "It's a nickname from back in my SEAL days. Long story. If you're finished, I'll clean up our food and take you home."

Panic seized her. "I have my own car," she said in a rush. "It's just right outside. I'll clean everything up and head out. I'm sure you have stuff to do, or, you know, it's late. You must be tired and ready to get home yourself."

"I've been away all day, but I do have some stuff to do here. But I think I am going to call it a day anyway. I'll walk you to your car, and I don't expect you to show up here tomorrow before ten."

"You don't have to walk me, Tristin. I can take care of myself."

His smiled widened. "I don't doubt that for a minute. I'm walking you to your car anyway."

She couldn't hold back her smile any longer. Together, they cleaned up their dinner. Kat logged out of the computer system and preceded Tristin out of the door. She felt a need to fill the silence between them and restore some sort of rapport.

"Is there anything specific you need me to work on tomorrow? I think I've done about as much as I can with your cybersecurity."

Tristin studied her, smiling as if he knew exactly what she was up to. "Yeah, I have some employees I need deep background checks on. We're hoping to employ them as investigators. I'll have Brick bring you the employee files in the morning."

"Brick?"

"Another nickname. His real name is Mason, but he probably won't answer if you call him that."

"Oh, I get it. Brick. Mason. Cute," she responded.

Tristin chuckled. "No. His nickname has nothing to do with his real name. At least as far as I know. Believe me, you'll understand his nickname when you see him."

They stepped off the elevator and crossed the lobby before either of them spoke again. Her car sat just where she'd left it earlier, and she was thankful she had stored her things out of sight in the trunk after she'd cleaned up that morning. She used her key fob to unlock the door.

"Thanks for escorting me, though it was unnecessary. I'll see you tomorrow."

Tristin didn't seem to hear her. He was busy looking over her car like it was something he'd never seen before.

"Is there a problem?"

"Remind me to have Callie give you an advance on your salary. You need reliable transportation."

"Callie? I thought she was the receptionist or office manager or something."

"Payroll and human resources are among her many duties at KSI. I'll have her include the advance in your contract she'll have you sign tomorrow," he explained as his gaze rested on her.

"I assure you an advance isn't necessary. This car may not look like much, but it is very reliable."

"Hmmmm, I'm not so sure. Give me your cell phone."

"What? Why?"

"I want you to text me when you get home, so I know you made it safe and sound in this deathtrap. To text me, you need my number."

"I can put your number in my phone myself. And my car is not a deathtrap."

He leaned against the car, his arms crossing over his broad chest, looking as if he had all the time in the world. "Phone."

She pulled her burner phone from her pocket. If he wondered why she had a simple cell versus the more high-tech smart phones, he kept it to himself. Thank goodness, since she'd rather not explain how she saved much needed money by using the simple pay-as-you-go phone. He rattled off his number, and she programmed it into her device before sending him a text. She heard the distinct buzzing from his pocket.

"Now you have my number. Goodnight, Tristin."

"Text me when you get home. See you tomorrow, Kat."

He pushed off her car as she climbed inside. He watched her as she drove away. Kat told herself not to look back, but she couldn't resist a glance in her rearview mirror to see he hadn't moved. Oh, he was gorgeous. She was in way over her head with him. How would she be able to work for him when she wanted to throw herself into his arms?

Kat had already decided where she would park her car for the night. She'd spent all day setting up security for KSI, including strategically positioning the cameras placed around the building and in the parking lot. She purposely left one section of the parking lot in the cameras' blind spots. She would be able to park there without fear of someone reporting her car. Tristin said he was heading home, and she drove around Grayson Cove for a half hour, giving him plenty of time to leave. Then she headed back to take her spot for the night. She set the alarm on her phone, giving her plenty of time to head to the truck stop to clean up for her second day at work.

While she was killing time, she stopped at an all-night service station to change into sweats and pull her blankets from the trunk. Once she was safe in her parking spot at KSI, she climbed into the back seat and pulled out her phone which she'd charged while she was at work.

"I'm safe. Goodnight, Tristin." There was so much she wanted to say, but she finally decided the simple text was best.

She didn't have long to wait for his response. *"I'm glad. C U 2moro, Katarina."*

She smiled before she tucked the phone into her pocket. She settled down into the cramped backseat, making sure her pepper spray was within reach. Sleep wasn't long in coming, and she drifted away into the passionate dreams featuring her boss in the starring role.

Chapter Six

Tristin had a plan.

After a night of tossing and turning, he finally rose at an early hour to go for a run. Watching the sunrise as he pushed his body with the strenuous exercise, he gained a new perspective. He knew what he needed to do.

He showered and dressed in record time, anxious to get back to the office. Building a new company meant navigating some bumps in the road. The situation he put himself in by suddenly hiring Kat and ignoring everyone's protests was one particular pothole he needed to repair. And he had to begin with a conversation with his staff. He would address Callie, Brick and Jay all at once. A talk with his brother would come later.

He craved coffee, but he didn't bother to make it before he left home or to stop at a coffeehouse on his way to KSI. Callie usually had coffee and baked goods waiting on him when he arrived. Maybe talking to his staff over breakfast would ease the tension. He was just glad he had Kat coming in later, and she would miss any conflicts.

He had no sooner pulled out of the driveway of his house than an incoming call came through on his Bluetooth system.

"Well, this is a surprise. To what do I owe the honor of this phone call, brother?"

"Shut it with the sarcasm, Tryst. I'm calling to make peace."

"Why the sudden change of heart?" Tristin goaded him, not ready to let the matter go.

"Your girl is good. I went in early to see what damage she did to the system. I figured I'd have my work cut out for me getting everything back on track. She was already there and showed me everything she had set up. Kat's impressive, Tryst."

"Wait," Tristin interrupted him. "She's at the office already?"

"Yeah," Travis confirmed. "Jordan said she was waiting on him when he showed up to unlock the building. She couldn't figure out how to use her keycard to get in, or she would have been in the command center before he got there."

"Dammit," Tristin grumbled. "I told her not to come in so early."

"What do you mean?"

Tristin filled his brother in on how Kat worked through her lunch break and how she stayed long after the rest of the employees went home. He gave the details of his conversation with her, leaving out the specifics of the kiss they shared.

"That girl is going to work herself into an early grave," he continued to rant.

Travis chuckled, only adding to his brother's ire. "Since when do you care if your employees are workaholics? You're starting a business, Tryst. You need people as dedicated to this as you are."

Travis spoke with the voice of experience, having spent years building the fitness center to meet his vision.

"I need my employees to work hard, not work themselves to death. It was her first day, and no one took the time to explain the job to her. All the work she did, she did on her own. She deserved to sleep and come in late this morning. In fact, that's exactly what I told her to do."

"Well, I'm telling you to cut her some slack. The last thing you need is to drive away the best computer analyst you're likely to find around here. She's just what you need for KSI." Travis' praise filled Tristin with pride, as if he had something to do with Kat's skills.

"Thanks, brother. Glad to see you came around to my way of thinking. Want to grab a beer or something later?"

"What? No date with one of your bed bunnies? Or did you get enough of that last night?" Travis teased.

Tristin rolled his eyes as he pulled into the KSI parking lot. He didn't need Travis reminding him of his lack of a social life as of late. Finding voluptuous women to warm his bed usually wasn't a challenge. He'd learned early on how to use his charm and good looks to win over any woman he wanted, and being a Navy SEAL only added to his appeal. Lately, the conquests have taken a back seat to his work. Perhaps that's why he felt on edge. He needed to get laid. The strange thing was he had no desire to find a random woman to scratch his itch.

"Tryst? You still there?"

Tristin hadn't realized he'd zoned out until his brother spoke. "I'm here. Look, it was late when I left work, and I just went home and crashed. I would be up for a beer if you want to hit Torch to-night."

"See you at seven, brother."

The call ended, but Tristin hesitated before heading inside, becoming lost in his thoughts again. He knew a batch of former SEALS who could take great enjoyment if they knew of his dry spell, but he couldn't bring himself to care. Was he finally getting tired of the seduction game? Travis often teased him the day would come when his endless string of women would get old, but Tristin always denied it. In fact, he tried to convince his twin to join him in the pursuit. Travis wasn't a player, though he did have his fair share of dates with the occasional girlfriend. Travis built relationships while Tristin steered clear of them.

Unbidden, Kat's face swam into his mind's eye. She was just his type – beautiful, intelligent, independent. But she shared more common interests with Travis, starting with their love of computers that Tristin wouldn't even pretend to understand. Hell, they both even wore glasses. Would Travis be interested in Kat? The idea did not sit well with Tristin at all.

He exited his car and made his way inside with swift steps. He greeted Jordan but didn't stop for their usual small talk. He hoped Callie had the staff waiting on him for the meeting he called. He was ready to settle the matter of Kat's employment and get on with the business of building his company. He needed no more distractions.

"You're here," Callie greeted him when he stepped off the elevator. "Give me a moment, and I'll have your coffee ready."

"Forget it," he grumbled. "Is everyone in the conference room?"

She blinked at his clipped tone. He and Callie had always enjoyed an easy rapport, and she'd been an asset in helping him start the business. This morning, he needed them all to see him as their employer and not as their easygoing colleague, and he decided to set the tone with his brisk manner.

"They were waiting until you arrived. Your voicemail indicated you would be nine o'clock coming in, and that's what time I told them to expect you. I can call them all together though. Most everyone is in their offices. I think Brick is in the command center, but I'm sure he can drop what he's doing to come to the meeting."

"Call them all to the conference room, and you join us too. Leave Kat and Jordan to do their work while we meet," he ordered before heading to his office. He took a moment to mentally prepare what he would say to them, and then he strode to the conference room.

Callie was already seated to the right of his chair at the head of the table. Sam came in, and Tristin took a moment to welcome the man as the newest member of the Alpha Team. Jay and Brick soon followed. Once they were all seated, Tristin rested his gaze on each one before he spoke.

“I appreciate the work you’ve all put in to get the company off the ground. I know I was MIA most of the day yesterday, but I’m pleased to announce I made a second hire while I was gone. Zane Wilder agreed to join us as the third member of the Alpha Team. He’s former Army, a sharpshooter. He’ll start next week. I have in mind to hire two others, and the team will be complete.”

“Look forward to meeting him,” Jay returned in a measured tone, his expression revealing nothing of his emotions.

“I’ve got Kat doing background checks on some potential investigators. It usually takes a while, but with the references I checked, I have a good idea of who we’ll be adding soon,” Brick added.

Tristin nodded. “Just keep us posted, Brick. Now, to address my hire yesterday. I get that you had an issue with how I went about hiring Katarina Walsh. I value your opinions when it comes to building this company. To make this work, I need you all to be as dedicated to this process as I am. But while I respect your input, I need to make myself clear on one point. I don’t expect you to agree with every decision I make. I do expect you to abide by them. The decision to hire Kat was mine and mine alone. She doesn’t deserve to be on the receiving end of your disagreement with me. Kat is a part of this team.”

“Tristin, we were only watching out for you,” Callie spoke up. “You had many good candidates for the job lined up to speak with you, and we had to cancel the interviews before they had a chance. We didn’t know anything about Kat. And from speaking with her this morning, she still doesn’t know everything you have in mind for her job.”

“I think she’ll handle it though, whenever you’re ready to loop her in,” Brick interjected. “She knows what she’s doing, man. And Travis told me this morning she’s good. You made a good choice with her.”

Callie fell silent, her face pinched with displeasure. Tristin waited for Jay to add his two cents, but the other man remained silent, studying Tristin with his unwavering gaze. Tristin decided now was the time to conclude the meeting.

"If no one has anything more to say, then you're dismissed."

Callie looked ready to say more, but clamped her mouth closed instead. She rose to be the first one out the door. Sam and Brick followed behind her. Tristin regarded Jay, who kept his seat.

"You have something else to say?" Tristin challenged him.

"Your meeting was unnecessary. Kat has proven she deserves the job. She didn't need you running interference for her."

"I disagree, but it doesn't matter. Anything else you want to tell me?"

Jay sat in silence as a couple of seconds ticked by. "Yeah. I do, but we should go to your office."

"Just spit it out, Jay."

"Tryst, calm down. I'm on your side when it comes to Kat. But you need to see what I found on the security footage this morning."

Jay left the room, leaving Tristin to stand to his feet in a shocked stupor. The kiss. Tristin closed his eyes as regret shot through him. He never considered the security cameras set up at the office when he surrendered to his attraction to Kat. Jay checked the security footage every day, so he had to have seen the passionate kiss between him and his new computer analyst. All his credibility was shot to hell.

Tristin found Jay sitting in his desk chair. He started to read him the riot act, but Jay waved him over before he could. Jay had the video cued and waiting on the computer. As soon as Tristin stood behind him, Jay clicked the mouse to play the footage.

An image of the empty KSI parking lot appeared, and the time stamp indicated the hour was after he and Kat left last night. He started to question Jay when he suddenly saw it – Kat's compact car appeared on screen, driving to a section of the parking lot not visible on the camera.

"She came back last night. She didn't tell me. She texted me to say she made it home." Tristin spoke more to himself though Jay heard every word.

"I thought it was odd too. That's why I went to the travel agency across the street. I've been flirting with the office manager over there. It wasn't hard to get her to share with me their security footage from last night. Look." With a couple of clicks, Jay had a second video playing.

Tristin again watched Kat's car pull into the parking lot and pull into the section where his camera's blind spot was. She backed her car into a vacant spot. Soon the lights switched off. He could see some movement within the car, but the camera was too far away to pick up exactly what she was doing. With another click, Jay moved the video forward several hours. The time stamp indicated 6:30 this morning when the car pulled out of the parking lot.

"She came back just a few minutes before Jordan showed up," Jay said as he stopped the video.

"I don't understand."

"She spent the night in her car, Tryst. I walked out to the parking lot to look at it after I saw this. I'm guessing she's living in her car. She probably finds a place to park it every night then looks for some place to get ready every morning."

Tristin moved on wooden legs around the desk to drop his body into the chair across from Jay. Words failed him as he tried to process what he just learned.

"She's lucky no one's tried to break into the car and mess with her," Jay continued. "What she's doing is dangerous."

"I realize that," he grumbled. "Why didn't she say something?"

"She said she needed the job. She probably thought you wouldn't hire her if you knew she was homeless. I was planning to talk to her, but I wanted you to know first."

Tristin shook his head. "No. I'll handle it. Let's just keep this between me and you."

"How are you going to handle it?"

Tristin sighed, running a hand through his hair. "I don't know. Man, I don't know."

Silence stretched between them. Jay finally rose and left without uttering another word. Tristin just sat in the chair, his mind reeling from what he'd just seen and what he had to do.

Chapter Seven

"How's it coming?"

Kat pulled her glasses from her face and rubbed her hands over her tired eyes. She only found the energy to half-smile at Brick Coffey as his huge frame crowded into the command center.

"I've made some progress, but you gave me a lot of files to go through. Deep background checks take time, you know."

"Show me what you've got so far."

She turned her chair around to access a long table she'd set up to use as a workstation. She'd spread the files out into four distinct piles. Placing her hand atop each one, she explained her system to the investigator.

"This stack are ones I still have to check. This stack are the ones I've done some surface checks on, but I want to dig just a bit deeper to be sure. This stack are the ones I would not recommend based on what I discovered after a preliminary search, but all the information is there for you to make up your own mind. And this stack are the ones I felt were your strongest possibilities. And if I may be so bold, I added my favorite to the top of the stack."

Brick raised a surprised brow before picking up the top file from the strong stack. He flipped it open and perused the paperwork while Kat nibbled her bottom lip nervously.

"This one is your top pick? Isobel Garcia."

"I know you're thinking I put her on top because she's a woman, and I won't deny that I think you could use more women around here. But she is very badass. An Army Ranger. A stint in the CIA. I want to meet her," Kat breathed, drawing a grin from Brick.

"CIA, huh? I'm surprised you found much on her. Usually those guys redact their agents' info to protect them in the field."

Kat flushed. She hadn't been sure if she was allowed to break any rules in researching the potential employees, so she'd stayed above board until she saw Isobel Garcia's file. The more she read, the more she wanted to know. She was careful to cover her tracks, but she employed more of her hacker skills with Isobel's research than she had the others.

Brick eyed her intently. "Anything I should warn Tryst about?"

Kat shook her head vehemently. "Oh, no! And if there was, I'd tell him myself. I own up to my own decisions."

She felt pleased to see admiration shine in his eyes. "Good to know," he said. He stacked the files she'd completed into his arms and nodded in her direction. "Thanks for the good work, Kat. Good to have you on board."

He left her alone, and Kat found herself grinning ridiculously. She loved this job, and the icing on the cake was having someone praise her for the tedious work she'd spent her entire day completing. Today had gone smoother than yesterday. The staff seemed more open to having her here. Even Callie seemed more accepting though her manner was still reserved. She met Sam, who was new to the company as she was. He was nice and good-looking, in a boy-next-door kind of way. He wasn't as classically gorgeous as Tristin, but his presence put her at ease. She had a feeling he would be a friend, an ally she didn't really have right now.

Kat looked down at the files she still had to research before glancing at the clock on her computer monitor. It was close to quitting time, but Kat wasn't really in the mood to stop working. She had gone against Tristin's order and come in early this morning.

Honestly, what else was she going to do if she didn't come to work? She had no money to go for breakfast, and she had no place to park her car to wait without drawing attention.

She had been excited to find coffee and Danishes waiting on the employees, and she helped herself to one of each. When she was sure no one was going to eat anymore, she'd secretly squirreled away the leftovers. When her lunch hour rolled around, she left her desk as Tristin expected her to. She snatched a water from the break room refrigerator, promising herself she would purchase many for everyone to share once she got paid. Not wanting to be observed eating breakfast leftovers, she did take her car a short distance to a park, and she sat on a bench while she ate. The whole time, her thoughts were on her work, and after a half hour, she headed back.

Now, after a few minutes of indecision, Kat picked up the next file on her stack left to complete. *Just a couple more, and I'll call it a night.*

Kat never noticed the offices emptying nor the lights in the hallway switching off. One file led to another to another to another. Before she realized it, she had over half of the stack gone. The research was like a treasure hunt, and she felt excitement the more she discovered. She looked for anything and everything to help Brick with finding the right people to hire. She wanted Tristin's company to succeed, whether she stayed here very long or not. But she wanted to stay. She liked the work. She liked being a part of something from the beginning.

"Working late again. Why am I not surprised?"

She started, whirling her chair around to see Tristin standing just inside the door. His expression was unreadable, his blue eyes regarding her intently. His handsomeness took her breath away, but she sensed he was troubled. His broad shoulders slumped slightly, the lines around his mouth more pronounced. His spiky hair was disheveled, his jeans and golf shirt rumpled.

"I lost track of time," she explained lamely. "Um, are you all right?"

His fists plunged into his jeans pockets as he moved slowly toward her. Her body tensed, but she wasn't sure why. Something about Tristin's mood felt off. He seemed…disappointed? Disillusioned? She didn't know. She hoped she wasn't the cause of his mood, but the dread settling in her stomach had her doubting.

"It's been a rough day."

"I'm sorry," she said sincerely. "What can I do?"

He walked to the front of the command center and paced back and forth on the tile floor. She watched him, waiting for his response though the wait was difficult.

"I want you to know you can trust me with the truth," he finally said. He stopped pacing and pierced her with his darkening eyes.

"About what? What are you talking about?"

"Why did you need a job so bad? Let's start there."

"I was working out of my home, where I lived with my mom. We ended up having the sell the house, and it was hard to maintain a business without a place to work out of. I've been looking for a job ever since. When my possibilities were exhausted where I lived, I hit the road, looking for work in other cities. I was about to hit the road again when I heard about the vacancy here," she said, feeling panic rise up within her.

"And you've had no income since you lost your job?" he questioned.

"I had savings to get me by at first. Then I've picked up odd jobs to carry me through."

He leaned against the wall and crossed his arms over his broad chest. "Then why are you living in your car?"

Breath left her lungs in a whoosh. She dropped her gaze. How did he even know? Not that it mattered. Now since he knew, he was about to change everything. Just as she allowed herself to be excited about her job, he was about to let her go because she had no address. It was unfair, but she'd encountered it before. Being homeless made people uncomfortable, like it was a contagious disease they would catch just by being around her.

"Don't lie to me, Kat," he spoke forcefully.

She jerked her head up, fury lighting her dark eyes. "I have not lied to you. About anything. I just met you *yesterday*, and frankly, my life is none of your business."

"When you sleep in your car in my parking lot, then yes, it is my business," he snapped, sending Kat's anger to new heights.

"Then I won't sleep in your parking lot anymore. Problem solved."

"Dammit, Kat." He resumed his pacing, his hand pushing through his hair before he shoved both of them into his pockets. "You should *not* be sleeping in your car! You should have said something."

"You think I like sleeping in my car? Believe me, it's not my first choice, but it's my life at the moment. It's only temporary. Why are you taking this so personally?"

"How long, Kat? How long has this been going on?"

"I don't know. A while. I was moving around looking for work. Hotel stays get expensive, so one night, I decided to save a little money by sleeping in my car at a rest area. One night led to two. It was just easier. I only slept in the parking lot last night because after setting up your security system, I knew it would be a safe place to sleep. That's it. Now you know. Now, tell me something, Tristin. How does you knowing change things for me?"

Her words gave him pause. "What do you mean?"

She saw emotion swirling in his eyes, but she couldn't identify it. She just knew its intensity frightened her. Her mind remembered their kiss. Its mind-numbing effects kept her warm through the chilly night, and it made her believe things she shouldn't. She started to believe she was where she belonged. She started to believe Tristin was different. Believing meant she hadn't prepared herself for it all to blow up in her face.

"Forget it," she said, standing so suddenly her chair tipped precariously. She righted it before it could fall over. Then she gathered her cell and her bag and turned on her heel. Her anger made her steps hurried.

"Wait! Where are you going? Kat, wait! Dammit, wait!"

She didn't make it any farther than the door to the command center when Tristin grasped her arm to stop her retreat. She refused to look at him.

"Kat, please, don't walk away."

"What do you want from me?" she whispered.

"Your trust. That's all. I swear your job is secure here. Tomorrow, you're not to come into work until you find a place to live. Once you do, I'll advance you the money to cover the rent until you're back on your feet."

"I can't ask you to do that."

"You didn't," he murmured, his breath brushing against her cheek. "You are a part of this team now. We watch out for each other. We protect each other. I only want to help."

She raised her eyes. He stood close enough she could see every hue of blue within his irises. Her gaze drank in the gentle planes of his face. This man was too good to be true, and she realized just how desperately she wanted to trust him.

"Thank you," she finally told him, her tone breathless.

He reached up a hand. A finger stroked the side of her cheek, the callouses deliciously rough against her skin.

"I think it's time to call it a night. Do you have all of your things?"

She nodded, not trusting herself to speak.

"Good. Let's go. Jordan's already locked everything up, so we're good to go."

She blinked as he pulled away. "Go where?"

"You're staying with me tonight. I have plenty of space, and you'll have your privacy. I meant what I said, Kat. The days of you sleeping in your car are over."

"I can't. You're my boss. Everyone here is just now starting to accept me. What will they say if they knew I was staying with you? They'll get the wrong idea."

"No one has to know. You'll leave here in your car and follow me to my place. As far as Jordan is concerned, you and I just happen to be leaving at the same time. Jay knows you've been living out of your car, but I told him I would talk to you. He trusts you and I will work it out, so he won't say anything. Trust me, Katarina."

She melted. How could she trust him after only knowing him less than forty-eight hours? But she'd had to learn to rely on her instincts, and her gut told her Tristin Knight was a good man. Plus, the idea of sleeping in a bed instead of her back seat was too appealing to pass up.

"Okay. Thank you. I'll never be able to repay you for this."

He held her gaze for several heartbeats. She was mesmerized by the clear blue of his eyes.

"No repayment necessary. Let's go and get you settled for the night."

Taking a deep breath to slow her racing heart, she stepped out ahead of him into the hallway. She said a silent prayer for strength to handle whatever the night held in store for her.

Chapter Eight

What the hell was I thinking?

He was in too deep with Kat. He knew it, but he couldn't stop himself.

The moment Jay told him about Kat living in her car, Tristin slipped into a state of shock. There was no reason he would have known, but he'd beat himself up for not figuring it out. He walked her to her car the night before. He watched her pull away. He saved the text she sent him to let him know she was settled in for the night.

Tristin had taken all day to consider what to do or even say to Kat about her situation, but the only thing he knew for certain was he would not allow her to spend one more night in her car sleeping on the street or in a parking lot.

He strode into the command center fully expecting to put her up in a hotel until she found an apartment. Without realizing what he was saying, the idea of the hotel morphed into an invitation to stay at his home. He had plenty of space in the sprawling two-story fortress he lived in. But he could have all the space in the world, and it wouldn't be enough to keep him from feeling hopelessly drawn to Katarina Walsh.

Tristin tried to be cool about it. She wasn't the first woman to spend the night at his place. He offered to prepare a simple meal of grilled hamburgers and tried to add to the casual invitation by suggesting they watch a movie while they ate.

But he was anything but cool. She had finally acquiesced to staying with him, but he saw the doubt in her eyes, telling him she second guessed her decision. Even as he led the way to his home, he kept one eye on the road and one on the rearview mirror to make sure she followed him to his house without deciding to ditch him, driving out of town and out of his life.

And now, his body burned, and not from the heat from his barbecue grill. Even the chill of the night failed to cool his desire.

After he'd shown Kat around his house, she asked to shower while he prepared dinner. He'd been quick to say yes, wanting her to feel comfortable in his home, but he heard the huskiness deepening his voice. He'd instantly hardened, and images of Kat naked in the shower, the water slicing over her smooth skin, were pure torture.

Tristin had been instantly attracted to women before. Hell, his nickname described his track record with the opposite sex. He never had difficultly charming any woman he wanted. Most of them he had convinced to simply spend the night warming his bed, and then walk away the next day. He'd had a couple he'd dated for longer than one night, but no one ever snared him in a long-term relationship. No one ever made him wonder what it would be like to have one.

Within the span of a couple of days, Katarina Walsh evoked in him intense, foreign emotions. She had him looking forward to making her smile or hear her talk non-stop about computer stuff he didn't understand. She had him imagining what it would be like to have her in his home permanently.

Tristin pulled the burgers from the grill and carried them inside to the kitchen. He busied himself with slicing a tomato, the only vegetable he had in his refrigerator. He wasn't sure if she wanted cheese on her burger, so he just placed a couple of singles on the plates just in case. He reached for a couple of bags of potato chips in various flavors. When he turned from the cabinet, he froze as his eyes lighted on Kat standing in his kitchen. She dried her silky hair and brushed it until the sable locks shone. Her face was freshly scrubbed and lovely. She dressed in well-worn jeans and a plain T-shirt. Her bare toes peeked from under the hem of her jeans, and Tristin's mouth went dry. He'd never considered toes to be sexy, but *damn*, if he wasn't turned on by Kat's bare feet.

"Everything looks delicious," she said. Everything about her was soft and beautiful.

Tristin gulped. "Have a seat at the table. Unless you've changed your mind about that movie? Want a beer or water? That's about all I got to drink."

"Water's good, and I think I'd rather eat at the table if that's all right."

He placed the plates on the table before grabbing their drinks from the refrigerator – water for her and beer for him. "I wasn't sure how you wanted your burger, so if there's something else you want, let me know."

"This is great. Thank you, Tristin."

"It's really no problem."

They ate in silence for several minutes. Tristin racked his brain for something intelligent to say, but he couldn't think straight with Kat sitting this close to him. Her scent swirled around him, filling his senses with the most seductive aroma. He was losing his mind with his attraction for her, and he realized he didn't really care.

"Your house is amazing," Kat finally said. "So much space for just one person."

"I don't plan for it to be just me forever," he surprised himself by admitting.

She leaned back in her seat to regard him thoughtfully. "Really? What do you mean?"

He shrugged, now embarrassed to have brought up something personal.

"Come on. You can tell me. I promise your secret and your rep are safe with me," she said lightly.

"My rep? You've known me for two days. What would you know about my rep?"

"Your nickname is Tryst. Surely you didn't think I wouldn't ask questions about it. Just so you know, the guys at work take way too much pleasure in telling stories about your sex life."

Tristin squirmed. His lifestyle was his choice, but hearing Kat speak about it flippantly made him wish he hadn't bragged so much to Jay and Brick. Military guys could gossip worse than teenage girls.

Kat looked down at her plate. "Never mind. We can talk about something else. I didn't mean to get too personal."

He exhaled loudly. "It's fine. You can ask me anything. If I don't want to talk about it, I'll tell you. And unfortunately, the stories you've heard about my reputation are probably only slightly exaggerated. I had a very demanding military career, and now I'm building my own company. I haven't wanted to complicate things with anything more serious than one-night stands. That's just the way it's been."

Kat chewed another bite of her hamburger as she regarded him. "You don't have to justify your choices to me. I'm not judging. You've been great to me, and I guess I'm a little curious about you."

"That makes two of us. I'm curious about you too."

"Okay. How about for tonight only, I answer a question of yours, and you answer a question of mine?"

He pierced her with his stare. Opening up to her was treading on dangerous ground. All his instincts were screaming for him to run, to keep as much distance as possible between them. But the chance to know more about her was too hard to resist.

"Okay," he agreed. "First to answer your question. I built this house thinking I'd one day find a woman I'd want to marry, and we'd fill the spare rooms with kids. The security system I had installed is state-of-the-art. I designed it myself with my future family in mind."

He pushed his plate away and rested his arms on the tabletop. "Do you have any family, someone you could have stayed with instead of living out of your car?"

Now it was her turn to push her plate away and sigh. "My mother lives in a special care facility, so no, I couldn't stay with her. I did, for a while, but we had to sell the house to help pay for her care. If anything, she's part of the reason why I was desperate to find a job. My brother pays for her care, but he lets me know on a regular basis I need to step up and help with that responsibility. We don't speak to each other unless we have to, and when we do, he spends the time reminding me what a loser I am because I don't have a job and I've left him to take care of Momma. He's an ass and has been our whole lives. He was not an option for me either.

"Why would you need a state-of-the-art security system for your family? What are you protecting them from?"

"That's two questions," he replied, buying himself some time. He needed to read her into the nature of his company if he planned to have her stick around. He hadn't expected now to be the time to do that. "I'm protecting them from me. Or my job rather."

Kat nodded. "I never thought PI work would be that dangerous. I mean, I'm sure it is for you and the other investigators, but not so much for the people in your lives."

"And you would be right. But KSI isn't specializing in just PI work. Brick has had you doing background checks on potential employees. You know they are all former military special ops. For one reason or another, they have stepped away from their military careers, but I want to give them opportunities to keep using their skills to help people."

"How so?"

He smiled at her genuine interest. "We'll have teams to hire out for special cases government agencies can't take on for various reasons. Jay is putting together the first of those teams, and we call it the Alpha Team. I want to have more, but until we can get the word out about what we do, I'll start small. We want to keep that part of the business classified to protect everyone. We will take on standard private security and private investigation cases too. Brick is putting the private security business together for us."

"Wow. That's…I don't know what to say, but wow."

"Now it's your turn," Tristin said. "To answer a question. Are you planning to stick around to help me build my company?"

She met his gaze, and he wondered at the flush creeping up her neck into her cheeks.

"I don't see how I can help exactly. I mean once I finish the background checks, I'm not sure what else there will be for me to do."

"We need technical analysts to help research cases, and I want them to provide support for the special ops teams in the field. I want to set up communication between the teams and the command center. If they could have someone pulling satellite images, they would know of dangers lying ahead and could respond. Or run facial recognition on a target to give the team a heads up of who they might be dealing with. So, with your skills, there would be plenty for you to do. I just need to know if you're in for the long haul."

"Do you want me to be in this for the long haul?"

"Yes. But if this is too overwhelming for you, I understand. You wouldn't be able to talk about it with anyone outside of KSI because the special ops side of the company will only be known to select clientele. Anonymity is key to protecting my teams."

Tristin moved to the chair right beside her. He rested a hand on her arm, his eyes holding hers. "Kat, you belong at KSI. I can't explain how I know, but I do. I just need to know if you're in this to stay or if this is just a stop on the way to something else."

"I don't know," she whispered. "I haven't thought too far ahead. My first priority is making enough to pay for a place to live and to send some money to my brother to help cover my mothers' expenses. I can't promise more than that right now."

Tristin traced a finger down the side of her face, the silkiness of her skin making him wonder if she felt just as smooth all over.

"I understand," he said softly. "I'll help you to get back on your feet, whether you decide to stay with KSI or not. But make no mistake. I want you to stay."

"Tristin," she whispered.

Her brown eyes darkened with desire, something he felt stirring within him. His nerve endings hummed. He couldn't remember the last time he wanted someone as much as he wanted Kat. His palm cradled her cheek before sliding into her silky hair. Her lips parted slightly, and he swallowed a groan. He needed to stay away from her. He felt too much where she was concerned, and he was on dangerous territory. But knowing what he should do and actually doing it was a distinction his brain couldn't make.

"You should run," he said instead. "Because I'm about to kiss you, and if that's not what you want, now would be the time to pull away."

"I can't. Because I want that too."

Her words broke the last of his resolve. He grasped the back of her head and pulled her forward, their lips connecting in an explosive kiss. She whimpered as his tongue plundered her mouth, her taste clouding his senses. Without breaking their kiss, he grasped her arms and pulled her closer until she settled on his lap. Her sweet ass rubbed deliciously against his groin. He wrapped his arms around her to hold her tightly in place. His palm slipped under her shirt to feel the smooth skin at her waist.

She felt right. She fit in his arms and against his body better than he could have imagined. Her warmth seeped through his clothes and lit him on fire. He needed her beneath him. He wanted to feel the length of her body against his. Shifting her until she straddled his lap, he held her close and stood. His lips trailed a path down to her neck as he carried her effortlessly to the living room. The couch provided the closest surface for him to have Kat as he wanted her.

Her hands found their way under his shirt, and he grinned at how she shoved the garment up, struggling to get it off. Reaching behind him, he yanked the shirt over his head to help her out. Her fingertips were light as they explored the planes of his torso. Tristin was ready to do his own exploring. He slid her shirt up, his thumbs hooking into her simple bra to drag it up until it all bunched under her arms. Her full breasts bounced with their release. His mouth watered to see her nipples hardening under his perusal.

"God, you're perfect," he breathed. Then he claimed a pink nub, nipping it with his teeth before soothing the sting with a sweep of his tongue.

Kat released a gasp as her fingers tangled in his hair. He suckled one breast before moving to the other. Kat writhed beneath him as he traveled down her body, leaving a trail of hot kisses in his wake.

"Tristin! Please!"

He raised his head, and his eyes collided with hers in a heated stare. The lust was there in the fathomless depths of her gaze. She wanted him as much as he did her. Hell, he was ready to combust if he didn't claim her soon. He wanted to be buried inside her as she shattered in his arms. He leaned down until his lips hovered close to the delicate shell of her ear.

"I'm about to make you mine, Katarina. This is your last chance. If you don't want this, now's the time to speak up."

He held his breath waiting for her to choose. If she said no, he would walk away, but the move would likely kill him.

"I want this. I want you, Tristin."

His pent-up breath left him in a rush. He grinned as he shot up to his feet, pulling her up with him. Before she could react, he scooped her into his arms.

"Then we're doing this right." He marched to his bedroom as her slender arms clung to his neck.

He deposited her in the middle of his bed. His grin widened when she giggled as she bounced on his mattress. He placed his hands on either side of her thighs and slowly crawled his way up the length of her body. He kissed her with all the passion welling up inside him, and her fervor in returning his kiss almost had him coming in his pants. As much as he wanted to take things slow and savor every moment of his first time with Kat, he knew he'd never last.

He broke their contact so he could draw her jeans and panties down her shapely legs. He flung the garments to some spot on the floor behind him. He studied her lying gloriously naked, and he was awestruck. She blushed under his scrutiny. The sight of her dark hair spread on his pillow, her skin lustrous against the dark duvet, her scent swirling around him, burned into his memory.

"Tristin?"

He hated the uncertainty lacing her tone and clouding her eyes.

"You're beautiful, Katarina."

"Why do you do that?"

His gaze softened as he watched her. He wanted to touch her, to lose himself in her, but he wanted her ready. He needed her to be with him with no regrets.

"Do what, sweetheart?"

"You're the only one who uses my full name. Everyone I know calls me Kat except you."

He flicked open the button on his jeans and delighted in how her eyes smoldered with desire. "I call you Kat."

"You called me Katarina just now. You actually call me by my full name a lot." She intently followed his hand as he lowered the zipper slowly.

He spoke deliberately as he shoved his jeans and boxer briefs down his legs and kicked them to the side. "There are times when you're talking tech speak I don't understand or responding to something with your sarcastic wit, and Kat is the name that suits you best. Then there are times, like now, when your beauty takes my breath away, when looking at you makes me forget about everything except memorizing every shade of brown in your hair, every curve of your body and every sweet sound you make when I caress you – those times are when you are Katarina, the sexy siren I can't stop thinking about."

"Oh." Her lips formed a perfect oval, and Tristin couldn't hold back any longer.

He reached into the drawer of his bedside table for a condom, ripping open the package as if his life depended on it. He made quick work of rolling it over his cock, and before she could blink, he covered her body with his and gave her another soul-shattering kiss.

"As much as I want to take things slow, I can't, Katarina. I need to make you mine. *Now.*"

"Yes."

And with that, he thrust into her with one swift motion, a moan escaping him. Her slick channel gripped him, and Tristin paused to savor the exquisite sensation. She clutched him as if trying to draw him closer. She whimpered with her need, her hips bucking beneath him. Then he began to move, withdrawing gradually before slamming back into her until he couldn't tell where his body ended and hers began.

"Tristin! Please!" she cried, and Tristin increased his pace.

He pounded into her, the pressure building up within him. His eyes never left her face. As her body tightened around him, he knew her orgasm was close, and he continued his unrelenting pace. When Kat fell over the edge into the tsunami of her rapture, Tristin followed. His own orgasm ripped through him with a force that left him weak. They rode the wave of their passion together, and as they came down from the intensity of their orgasm, Tristin rolled to his side without pulling out of her. He gathered her close, dropping feather-like kisses to her brow. He needed to dispose of the condom, but with the feel of her next to him, sweat glistening on her skin, her breaths coming out in puffs from the exertion of their coupling, he loathed to leave her.

"You're amazing," she mumbled against his chest, the vibration traveling down to his toes.

He chuckled. "I was thinking the same of you."

"Tristin, I—"

"Shhh." If she was about to tell him how their moment changed everything and how she regretted giving in to their moment of passion, he couldn't bear to hear it. He regretted none of it. She was his. There was no turning back.

"Just sleep, Katarina. There will be time to talk later."

When, after a few moments, her breathing evened and her body relaxed, he eased away from her to clean up. He came back to the bed and watched her sleep, smiling at how she curled into the warm spot he'd vacated. She never stirred as he lifted her to draw down the covers. He climbed in next to her, covering them with a sheet, and wrapped her in his embrace. With a contented sigh, she melted into him.

Peace stole over Tristin. Soon his eyes closed, and he drifted into a deep slumber.

Chapter Nine

The sun rose, and reality crashed in on Kat like high tide crushing a sandcastle. Her night in Tristin's arms replayed like a movie reel in her head, and she battled contradicting emotions ranging from utter bliss to complete terror. Sex with him was mind-blowing, but the connection she felt with him was even more intense. Another time at another place, she would have freely explored where the connection would lead.

But the time was now, and the place was her boss' unbelievable house. Sleeping with him made her vulnerable. If it all went south, she would lose her job again. She would be reduced to living out of her car again. She would be on the receiving end of her brother's elitist judgment. *Again.*

She wanted to savor the sweetness of waking up in Tristin's arms. The warmth of his body next to hers lulled her into a contented and lazy state. His breath stirred her hair, and she smiled. The moment was one she could grow accustomed to. She shifted within the circle of his arms, and her smile widened as she gazed into his face.

God, he's gorgeous! His hair was disheveled from a good night's sleep, and dark lashes fanned his cheekbones. Even relaxed, his mouth was kissable. Her skin warmed at the memories of how his mouth kissed her from head to toe. She might regret the consequences of succumbing to her attraction to him, but she would never regret having sex with him not once, not twice, but three times.

But those consequences. Not knowing what those would be is what drove her from Tristin's side. She would have pegged him as a light sleeper, but she was able to slip from his bed without waking him. She pulled on what clothes she had in the bedroom before padding on quiet feet to the living room to finish dressing. She needed time to herself, to sort through how she felt about what happened and to develop a plan for how to rebound when it all slipped from her fingers.

The hour was too early for her to retreat, and truthfully, she didn't want to leave Tristin. If he woke and found her gone, he would assume she freaked and ran away. Even if she left a note to explain otherwise, she didn't want to risk hurting him. She faced situations head-on, and this one was no different. She just needed time to sort through scenarios.

Kat wandered through the house, in awe over the space and the sleek decor. Her mind couldn't reconcile the playboy bachelor reputation Tristin carried with the lovely home he admittedly bought for the family he planned to have. There was much more to him than she knew – than most people knew, she suspected. She stopped at a set of glass doors in a room she guessed to be his office. The view over the sweeping valley behind his house, with the sun bursting through the sky in a breathtaking display of color, left her dazed. This place was more than a home. It was a sanctuary, a retreat from all the stresses and problems of life.

On a whim, she managed to drag a leather reading chair over in front of the doors. With her legs curled under her, she settled comfortably, and the peace of her surroundings stole over her. She could easily believe all was well in the world, that all would fall into place with her new job, with her family, and with whatever this was with Tristin.

The warm breath on her neck startled her, but then she sighed when Tristin's lips kissed the sensitive spot just below her ear. He settled his lean frame on the arm of the chair, taking her hand between both of his.

"You okay, baby?"

Kat's belly dipped at his endearment. "I'm fine. I just wanted a moment to myself. I hope it's okay I came in here. Your view is amazing."

He lifted her hand to kiss her palm. "The view is one reason why I bought the house. You sit here. I'm going for breakfast."

She uncurled her feet and started to stand. "I can make something."

Tristin placed a hand on her shoulder and gently pushed her back against the chair. "Nope. I'm not sure I even have anything for you to make, and there's a bakery not far from here. I'll only be gone a few minutes. You stay put and relax."

"Are you sure?" Kat felt uneasy being alone in his house.

He squeezed her hand. "I'm sure, babe. Just tell me how you take your coffee."

She smiled. "With cream and sugar. Thank you, Tristin."

The smile faded when Tristin left. Kat turned back to the glass doors, but the view no longer held her spellbound. She realized how easily she could fall for this man. From all she heard about him, he was the king of the one-night stand, but he didn't seem to want her to leave. She expected him to be offended by her need for solitude. Instead, he supported it and gave her space. She thought he'd send her packing when he found out about her situation, but instead he opened his home to her and seemed comfortable having her there. She wanted to believe she could finally relax, that her situation was taking a turn for the better, but she couldn't shake the feeling it would all be pulled out from under her. Again.

Her phone vibrated in her back pocket, startling her out of her musings. She shifted in the chair to pull the phone out. The groan and the eye roll were instinctual reactions to seeing her brother's name on the screen. Leave it to Nick to sense her vulnerable state and choose that moment to call and give her grief. Her finger hovered over the ignore button, but she couldn't bring herself to depress it. If something was up with their mother, she would never know if she didn't answer the phone. Nick didn't leave voicemails, and he was too old-fashioned to text.

"You're calling awfully early, Nick," she answered. "Is everything okay?"

"No, it's not okay, Kat." Nick Walsh's bark set her teeth on edge. Kat could already picture his long face ruddy with anger, and his dark eyes narrowing.

"Is it Mom? What's wrong?"

"What's wrong is you owe me money. I can't keep shouldering this responsibility by myself, Kat. You have to step up. Mom's been asking for you, and you don't know how hard it is for her to know you've run off."

Kat sat up straighter, her own anger bubbling up. "Is that what you told her? I ran away? What the hell, Nick? I didn't run away. You sold my home remember? I moved so I could find work and afford a place to live. Why would you make Mom believe that?"

"What else was she supposed to think, Kat? You sure haven't called to explain what was going on."

Kat sighed. Her brother knew perfectly well why she hadn't called their mother. As Lori Walsh's dementia progressed faster than any of them expected, Kat never knew if her mom would know who she was or remember anything she said.

"I just started a new job in Grayson Cove. I'm not too far away, Nick. I'm looking for an apartment today, and once I'm settled, I'll be there to visit. Please tell Mom, OK? Don't let her think I'm running from her."

Despite what she asked of him, Kat realized Nick could tell

their mother anything he chose. He was the one who lived close by and paid the bills. Until she returned, he had the control.

"You still owe me for Mom's living expenses. When can I expect a payment, Kat? Since you finally have a job."

"As soon as I can, Nick. I should go. I have a big day ahead. Please tell Mom I'll visit soon." She ended the call before she had to listen to him anymore.

"Are you all right?"

Kat jumped from the chair and whirled around to face Tristin. Her heart pounded from his sudden reappearance.

"Oh, you startled me. I didn't realize you were back." She purposely avoided his question. She wasn't all right, but she didn't want her family drama to drag down her time with Tristin.

His lips quirked in a sexy half-smile that weakened her knees. "Just walked in. Do you want to just sit in here while we eat? It's more comfortable."

"Oh," she exclaimed. Her head turned from him to the view over her shoulder and back to him. "Do you mind? I really like it in here."

"Sit. I'll be right back."

He disappeared, and Kat went to work dragging another chair over next to hers. She situated them where both had a great angle to watch the view from the glass doors but could also see each other as they talked. She moved an end table over between the two chairs to give them a place to put the food and coffee. Pleased with her redecorating, she beamed at him when he came back with his hands ladened with their breakfast. His step faltered as he stared at her. Kat wrung her hands nervously.

"I'm sorry. I promise I'll move everything back."

"No, no, it's fine. Move whatever you want. It's just…"

"What? What's wrong?"

"Nothing. It's just you're beautiful when you smile. You sort of took my breath away."

She lowered her eyes as a blush stole over her skin. "Wow. You sure know how to romance a lady, Mr. Knight."

"Just speaking the truth, Miss Walsh." Tristin settled a tray of muffins and pastries on the table before handing her an extra-large coffee. "I wasn't sure what you like, so I bought a bunch of different stuff. Help yourself."

They sat, and Kat couldn't resist sinking her teeth into a gooey chocolate pastry. "This is great. Thank you."

"You're welcome." They ate in silence for several minutes, Tristin looking out to the backyard and Kat studying him.

"You don't fool me, you know."

He grinned but didn't look at her. "I don't know what you're talking about."

"You want everyone to think you're some player who changes girlfriends more than you change your underwear. I don't buy it," she said around a mouthful of breakfast. "I think you're secretly a romantic underneath your tough exterior."

"And if I was? Would you like that about me?"

She returned his grin. "Possibly. My question, though, is why? Why play the role of the playboy when you're not?"

His expression grew serious as he met her eyes. "It's not a role. I have dated a lot."

She regarded him intently. "No one serious?"

"One or two who I thought could be, but it never worked out."

"Why not?"

Tristin shrugged. "I'm not sure."

Kat's eyes narrowed, and she gave an unladylike snort. "Yeah, right. Spill it, Knight. Give me all the dirty details."

"You can't really want me to talk about my love life." He shifted uncomfortably in his seat.

She smirked. "Oh, but I think I do."

"Okay. I'll tell you. Then you have to tell me who called you and upset you this morning."

"Fine, but you spill first."

"I don't know what you want me to say. I date a lot, but I haven't had time for anything serious. And the women I've dated never wanted anything serious."

"But you said there were one or two…"

"Who were interested in my money and not me."

"You have a lot of money? I wouldn't have guessed," she teased as she waved her hands to indicate her stunning surroundings.

"My parents made sure Travis and I had what we needed to pursue what we wanted. It's opened doors for me, but it's not who I am."

Kat blinked at his honesty. "Are you close to your parents?"

"For the most part. They retired to Florida, and I don't see them as often as I'd like. They're great though."

"Tell me about them."

"Nope. It's your turn to talk."

Kat sighed. "Right. The phone call. There's not much to tell. It was Nick, my older brother."

"Tell me."

Her head tilted slightly as she looked at him curiously. "You don't want to hear about my family drama."

"I want to know more about you, Katarina."

There he goes again. Using her full name, the sound of it from his lips making her heart flutter. This man was dangerous on many levels.

"Nick and I have never been close. I was a late-in-life baby.

My parents were in their forties when they found out they were expecting me. Nick had been the only child for a long time, and I think when I came along, he didn't know how to feel. He's fourteen years older than me, and he's always been more like a parent than a sibling. We're different. He sees me as a flighty, fly-by-the-seat-of-my-pants kind of person, and I'm really not. No matter what I do though, he won't change his mind about me. We fight a lot, and it breaks my heart he's the one watching after my mom. He's lying to her about me, and I can't do much about it."

"What about your dad?"

"He died when he was fifty-five. Heart attack. I was fifteen, and Nick was twenty-nine and already married. Nick's wife makes me think of a Stepford wife. Brenda's an accessory for Nick, but she seems content. It's not the type of marriage we grew up around. Mom and Dad were high school sweethearts and affectionate and loving with each other. That's the kind of marriage I want. Sometimes I wonder how Nick and I came from the same parents."

"You've never been married?"

She snorted, drawing a grin from Tristin. "Uh, no. I can't seem to keep my own life on track for anything more complicated than finding a job. I've dated a few people, but it's been all about my career, then taking care of my mom, then keeping Nick off my back."

"Let me help you," he said, reaching for her hand. She tried to draw back, knowing her fingers were sticky from the Danish, but he wouldn't relinquish his hold.

"You are helping me. The job and the advance and a place to crash until I can find something more permanent. I'll never be able to repay you for taking a chance on me." Her tone became hushed, though she wasn't sure why. It was as if she would shatter the intimacy of the moment if she spoke any louder.

"How much do you owe your brother? I can give you enough to pay him back," he offered.

She shook her head vehemently, her hair whipping against her face until she shoved the locks back. "No. I'm not taking any more money from you. You're helping me pay for a place to live. That's enough. Now, it's your turn. Tell me about your family. Hopefully they're more drama free than mine."

He studied her for a moment before allowing the change in subject. "For the most part, yeah, I'd say they're drama free. Let's see, Dad owned his own business. A bunch of hardware stores may not seem like much, but they were very successful. Mom was a schoolteacher. They met when she came into Dad's flagship store wanting to buy some supplies for a class project her students were working on. He donated all of the supplies hoping she'd agree to go out with him."

"And did she?"

"Nope," Tristin said with a grin. "Mom said Dad seemed full of himself, so when he asked her, she turned him down. He kept asking her out for like a month, and she turned him down every time. She said she felt like she presented a challenge to him he couldn't pass up, and she didn't want to be someone's challenge."

"Wow. I think I'd like her."

"You would, and she'd like you too. Both of you are stubborn and beautiful."

Kat's jaw dropped. She wanted to say something, but she wasn't sure if she should protest his assessment or be flattered. He grinned as if he knew of her internal battle. He continued before she could make up her mind.

"Dad finally stopped asking Mom out, and she said she realized she started to miss him. She went by the store and saw him talking to a woman, who kissed him on the cheek. She was sure she'd lost her shot with him. My mom, being who she is, went up to Dad, apologized for not giving him the benefit of the doubt, and offered to be his friend. Dad explained the woman Mom saw kissing his cheek was my Aunt Linda – Dad's sister. They shared a laugh and ended up going out on their first date. A month later, they eloped."

"Wait. They got married after dating a month? That's a little soon, isn't it?"

Tristin shrugged. "Dad said he wasn't willing to risk losing her, so he fast tracked their romance. My dad can act impulsively sometimes, but his instincts are always spot on. Just when his stores were doing well, he sold them to a franchise that wanted to capitalize on his success. Dad made enough money for him and Mom to retire to Florida, and he set up trusts for me and Travis."

"I always thought fathers dreamed of leaving their business empire to their sons."

"Dad knew we had no interest in running the hardware stores. I wanted to enlist, and Travis joined the police academy. He made it up the ranks to detective quickly, but he got burned out on the job. He decided to open up the gym."

"And you became a Navy SEAL," she filled in the blanks. "How did you go from serving your country to starting KSI?"

Tristin grew somber. "My SEAL team and I were on a mission in Afghanistan. We had our targets in sight and were ready to move in. Something about it was off. My gut kept telling me to go back, but our Intel was solid. I ordered my team to move ahead. There was a group of local insurgents who attacked us. We didn't see them coming. My entire team was injured. We're fortunate we didn't lose anybody. We were sent home on a furlough to recuperate."

"Oh, Tristin, I'm sorry. Were you badly injured?"

"I was pretty banged up. I spent a couple of weeks in the hospital and then a few months in rehab. I got word then that they were splitting up my SEAL team. We were all being reassigned, and I was no longer going to head up my own team. I decided retirement seemed a better choice."

"Wow. That had to be a tough decision for you. Do you regret it?"

"Yes and no. I miss being a part of the team, but I didn't really trust myself after what happened. I felt sorry for myself for a while. Travis finally convinced me to help him set up his gym and get it off the ground. Working with him got me to thinking about starting my own business. My commanding officer was the one who planted the idea of KSI in my head, and I approached Jay about it. His team was the reason my team made it out of Afghanistan alive, but I knew he wasn't planning to reenlist. We got to talking over beers one night, and before I knew it, we had the entire business plan for KSI written out on bar napkins. I told him I wasn't interested in going into business with a partner. My dream was to run my own business. He was fine with it. He just wanted to run a team and help people. It was the perfect partnership"

"Amazing," she breathed. "And now I get to be a part of it too. I love the job already, but now I'm really excited to be working at KSI. Thank you for giving me the opportunity."

He squeezed her hand. "I'm glad to have you a part of this too. I don't want you to worry. Whatever happens with us has nothing to do with your job at KSI. I promise."

Kat smiled, but she couldn't ignore the seed of doubt nibbling at the back of her mind. Tristin couldn't predict the future, nor could he predict the fallout if their affair ended badly.

"And speaking of KSI," Tristin said as he rose to his feet. "I'd better shower and head into the office. We're interviewing potential team members today, and Jay will kick my ass if I'm late."

He placed his hands on the arms of her chair and leaned his lithe body in close. His lips captured hers in a kiss meant to render her bones to mush. He drew away reluctantly and held her gaze.

"Sit here as long as you want. Make yourself at home."

He swaggered out of the room, leaving Kat in a daze, torn between the passion and the anxiety he stirred within her.

Chapter Ten

Tristin leaned against the back of his chair until the hydraulic mechanism underneath creaked. A satisfied smile rested on his lips, his eyes skirting over each of the file folders on his desk.

It's done, he thought, enjoying the satisfaction of all his plans coming together. He had the members of his first special operations team in place. With Jay leading them, Sam Montgomery, Zane Wilder, Brennan Beckett and Griffin Tyler would bring their own unique abilities to the Alpha Team. Each man was different in his background and his temperament, but both Tristin and Jay felt the team would only benefit from the differences.

He and Jay interviewed almost twenty different candidates to bring them to this team of five. Tristin envisioned the team comprising of veterans from different branches of the military, and he got his wish. Jay and Brennan – known by his initials "BB" – were former Navy SEALs, as he was, and Griffin was a former Air Force fighter pilot, which was why most people called him Wings. Zane and Sam were both Army veterans with Zane gaining a reputation as a sharpshooter and Sam as a Ranger.

Not only was his first special ops team in place, but he also had a staff of private investigators already hired. Brick decided to keep the staff small with just him, former Marine Alexander "Lex" Bishop and Isobel Garcia, a former Army Ranger and CIA agent who seemed very reserved and independent. Tristin had some doubt about hiring her, but Brick said she checked out.

Then there was Kat. Tristin's smile widened. Two weeks had passed since he discovered her living in her car, and she'd been staying at his place ever since. She continued her search for an affordable apartment, and each time she came close, Tristin vetoed the location due to security concerns or whatever plausible excuse fit the moment. His objections carried more half-truth than true concern, but they served to keep the beautiful computer hacker at his side and in his bed.

He was amazed at how easily they fell into a routine. Kat worked late most evenings, and she could spend a few hours in the mornings looking for a place to live. Tristin would stay late at the office as well, so he could walk her to her car as they left each evening. They would share a meal and relax in the TV room for a while before their passion ignited, driving them to the bedroom. He never realized how much he would love waking up with a beautiful woman in his arms, but since the woman was Kat Walsh, he wasn't surprised.

She was responsive to his touch, and he couldn't get enough of her. But more than that, he enjoyed having her snuggle into his side while they lounged on the couch. He was captivated with the light in her eyes when they talked about work and how the business was growing. Her laugh brightened his day, and her dry wit amused him. The more he was with her, the more he never wanted to be without her.

They managed to keep their relationship a secret from everyone but two people – Jay, who never missed anything, and Travis, who dropped by to invite his brother for breakfast one morning only to find Kat in Tristin's kitchen wearing only his T-shirt. He chuckled at the memory, but at the time they both worried about Travis' reaction to their relationship. Fortunately, his twin sensed how happy Kat made him and gave his complete support.

All the pieces of his life were coming together. Tristin didn't want to analyze it too closely, or he'd have to admit his run of luck couldn't last for long. Eventually Kat would find a place to live, and he wouldn't have an excuse to convince her not to take it. He would have a decision to make – let her go or admit to her he wanted to make a home with her.

A knock on his office door shook him out of his thoughts. Tristin raised his head to see Jay swagger inside and settle in a chair across from him. Jay jerked his chin toward the file folders on his boss' desk.

"What do you think?"

Tristin grinned. "I think we have our Alpha Team. We need to set up training."

Jay nodded. "Yeah, I thought of that. An old SEAL buddy of mine owns some mountain cabins up in the Rockies. I sort of explained what we had in the works." He held up a hand to silence Tristin's immediate protest. "I know. We agreed to keep the special ops team a need-to-know part of the business, but I trust this guy. Just hear me out.

"When I explained what we were setting up, he offered us his cabins to use for a training retreat. He's even agreed to set up some equipment and exercises for us to get in shape and start learning to work as a unit. He'll serve as a training facilitator. He's quoted a good price, Tryst, so I think we'd be crazy not to take him up on it."

"How much? And are you sure he's the one who should be training the team?" Tristin asked, and his eyebrows lifted as Jay shared a price well under what he expected.

"Judah Cavanaugh is more than qualified. His SEAL team was the one deployed for missions the government disavowed. His success rate puts everyone else's to shame. He's seen some tough shit, which is why he retreated to the mountains. He's not a fan of… people."

"Wow. Well, if he's willing and you trust him, then let's go for it. How soon can we set up the training?"

Jay rose, his lips twisted in an arrogant smirk. "This weekend. We fly up Friday and spend the week in the mountains. We can rent a plane, and Wings can do the flying. You in?"

Though he wouldn't actively serve on the team, Tristin had expressed his interest in being a part of the team's development from the get-go. He just didn't expect to have to leave Kat so soon.

"She'll still be here when you get back, Tryst. The time apart will do you good."

Tristin narrowed his gaze. "What are you talking about, Jay?"

Jay chuckled. "Come on, Tryst. You've fallen for Kat, and it's happened fast. You're worried things will change once you're out of town. If you ask me, she's fallen for you too. Even if she moves out of your house, man, she's not going very far. Besides, she would want you to do what you needed to for the company."

"I never said I've fallen for Kat or that I'm worried about anything," Tristin protested.

"You didn't have to." Jay walked to the door. "I'll set everything up with Judah. Just let me know if you decide to stay behind."

He turned to leave and bumped into Kat. She cried out, startled, as Jay caught her arms to steady her.

"Sorry about that. You okay?"

She released an exasperated sigh. "No, but it's not your fault. Sorry for running into you. Oh, and good morning."

She brushed passed him into Tristin's office. Jay turned to shoot a grin and a knowing look at his boss.

"Good morning to you, too, Kat," he drawled before disappearing down the hall.

His friend forgotten, Tristin rose from his desk to give his attention to Kat. Jay's words floated around in his mind, but he pushed them to the side. Instead he wanted to get to the bottom of whatever had Kat frustrated.

Kat deposited her laptop bag on the couch in his office before sinking into the cushions as if her legs could no longer support her. She rested her head on the back, a sleek braid sliding over her shoulder. She closed her eyes and adjusted her glasses on the bridge of her nose. Tristin couldn't hold back his smile as he watched her.

Was Jay right? Had he fallen for her? He didn't deny his thoughts were consumed with her. Before he met her, he looked forwarded to spending time at the office building his company. Now, the bright spot in his day was leaving work to spend the evening with her. He loathed to leave her side each morning, and the fact she immediately sought him out when she arrived at work today pleased him.

He settled on the coffee table across from her and took her slim hand between his. "Kat?"

"I'm. Never. Going. To. Find. A. Place. To. Live." Her words were clipped as they passed through her lips. She never moved as she spoke, her eyes staying closed.

"No luck today?"

Her eyes flew open, and she sat up suddenly, startling him. "No! None! I looked at apartments. I looked at houses to rent. I even looked at the cutest little house to buy. My feet are killing me, and it's not even lunchtime yet. It's been two weeks, Tristin. Why can't I find a decent, affordable place to live? Is that too much to ask?"

"You looked at a house to buy?"

And suddenly, the fire left her. He could see fatigue etched in her lovely face. She sighed, and his heart clenched. "Yeah. I knew I couldn't afford it, but I had this wild thought. It was such a cute house, very close to here, with two bedrooms, each with its own bath. I couldn't resist thinking what if…"

"What if?"

Her dark eyes captured his, and he hated the forlorn emotion in their depths. "What if Momma came to live with me. We could share the little house. I could hire a nurse to care for her during the day and in the evenings when you and I had plans. Then I'd know for sure how she was doing. She wouldn't have to live in some facility where strangers take care of her. She wouldn't be exposed to Nick's negativity all the time. I know most days she doesn't even realize what's going on, and truthfully, I can't afford a house of my own. But I indulged in the fantasy for a little while. I thought it would make me feel better."

"But it didn't." His hand caressed her cheek, and she tilted her head into his touch. "I'm sorry, sweetheart."

"It's fine," she said though her tone suggested otherwise. "I've tried to look on the bright side. I've been able to send some money to Nick, and he's stayed off my case. He's not called me since the first night I spent at your house, which I consider a good sign."

"Why don't you cut yourself some slack? Give yourself a break from the house hunting for a while. You're welcome to stay at my place for as long as you need to. I have to say I've enjoyed having a female roommate. Especially one as sexy as you."

His flirtations did the trick. A hint of a smile played across her lips. Tristin leaned in closer to plant a light kiss on her mouth.

"Thank you." Her soft, husky tone washed over him.

"For what, sweetheart? I haven't done anything."

"You've giving me a place to stay. You've been so understanding. I've never had someone to be there for me the way you have. Except for my parents."

He trailed a finger down her cheek to caress her neck. He smiled when her body shivered at the contact.

"Maybe we can go to visit your mom soon." The words left his mouth before he realized what he proposed, but he didn't regret the offer. After listening to Kat talk about her mom, he wanted to meet the woman who raised her.

"You, um, you want to go and visit… You want to meet my mother? Really?"

He grinned. "Yep. Mothers love me."

She giggled then sobered. "That's sweet, but most of the time my mom doesn't even know who I am. It'll be awkward and sad. I appreciate the offer, but you really don't have to."

Tristin leaned forward until his face was inches from hers. "Sweetheart, whatever you think is best is fine by me. But I wouldn't have offered to go if I didn't really want to meet your mom."

He kissed her. This time it wasn't a soft, simple kiss. It started out gentle but quickly grew more passionate. Tristin grasped her upper arms and pulled her to her feet. He wrapped his arms around her, drawing her close until her breasts pressed against his chest. His hands burrowed into her braid. He shouldn't kiss her, not in his office, not when they were keeping their romance a secret. But he couldn't resist her. She was his kryptonite, and he didn't care. Not as long as she stayed in his arms and by his side.

He loosened his hold when he felt her pull away, but he felt the loss of contact like a punch in the gut.

"We can't," she whispered. "I want to, but we can't."

"I know. I want to, but I know."

She regarded him for a moment before she gave him a slight smile. "I would love for you to meet my mom. Just say when, and I'll clear it with the facility."

He returned her smile. "Well, it'll have to wait a week or so. I'm heading out with the Alpha Team on Friday."

"What? You're leaving?"

He nodded. "Now that we have the Alpha Team selected, they

need to learn how to work as a team. Jay has a buddy who's going to run the training for them."

The smile left her face. "Yes, of course, you should be there. When do you leave?"

Tristin studied her closely. "Jay is setting it up for Friday. We'll be gone a week."

Kat started nibbling her bottom lip, and alarm bells sounded in Tristin's head.

"It's Okay, Kat. I won't be gone long, and you'll have some time to yourself. I'll call you as long as I can, but I'm not sure how cell reception will be where we're heading."

"It'll be weird," she muttered almost too low for him to hear her.

"What? Us being away from each other?"

"Me. Being alone. In your house."

Tristin wanted to chuckle, but he bit his lip to keep his mirth from spilling out. *Damn, she's adorable.* There wasn't a single thing about Katarina Walsh he didn't find enchanting, but he guessed his sentiments were the last thing she wanted to hear right now.

"I don't think it's weird. I like the idea of you watching after things while I'm gone. And in the meantime, we can enjoy being together until I leave."

She took a couple of steps back and then turned to walk to his office window. He followed her, wanting to know what bothered her – because it wasn't being alone in his house. He stopped several steps behind her, wishing she'd face him. Not seeing the emotions playing across her face was killing him.

"It's too soon. It's all so fast," she mumbled.

"What, baby? What are you talking about?"

She whirled around, her eyes frantic. "Us, Tristin. Just over two weeks ago, you hired me for a job I really needed. Then I go to your house, just to spend a night in a safe place. And I end up sleeping with you. We've been together ever since. We're hiding our affair from everyone. Hell, we're basically shacking up."

"Shacking up?"

"Stop teasing. I'm serious. We barely know each other. And you tell me you're going away, and I'm house-sitting for you like I'm… Like I'm…. Like I'm your girlfriend."

He caressed her cheek again. He'd never get tired of the feel of her silky skin against his fingertips.

"I actually like the sound of that," he admitted.

"You do? But it's fast. And you don't have girlfriends."

He encircled her waist with his arms and drew her close. "Hearing you being called my girlfriend feels right. It is fast, but I trust my gut. My gut tells me whatever this is between us is worth pursuing. I can't promise where it'll lead, but I'm more than willing to find out if you are. It's scary as hell, but my gut says it's worth it."

She rested her forehead against his chest with a soft sigh. "Scary as hell. Yes, I agree. I'm terrified."

He ran his hand in comforting circles on her back. "We'll figure it out together, baby. All I ask is you give us a shot."

Tristin felt the vibration of her voice against his chest, but he couldn't understand what she said. With a finger under her chin, he raised her head until she looked into his eyes.

"What, sweetheart?"

"Okay. I want to give us a shot."

"Good." He dropped a kiss to her forehead. "Then tonight, we celebrate. I'm taking you out for dinner, so no late night at the office."

She smiled. "Then I guess I'd better get to work."

With one last lingering kiss, she pulled away to gather her stuff. He watched her leave his office, her scent swirling in the air around him. He stood there for several minutes, thinking on their conversation. He felt his relationship with Kat just turned a corner, but he wasn't exactly sure how or what it meant.

As excited as he was to have the plans for his company come together, he wished he didn't have to leave her.

Chapter Eleven

Kat knew one thing for sure. She didn't do well with long distance relationships.

Tristin and the Alpha Team had been gone for five days. Less than a week, and Kat was already beside herself with missing him. She spent the weekend in his house, feeling like an outsider playing pretend. They'd been together for a few weeks, but Kat was too afraid to delve too deep into where their relationship was heading.

The first couple of days of his absence, he called her every night. Once she heard his voice, her insides melted, and all her doubts faded away. The hour was always late, and he sounded exhausted. But still they talked about anything and everything until neither could keep their eyes open. Kat would sleep contentedly through the night. Then the sun rose, and her doubts returned.

So, she kept busy. She cleaned until every surface of his house shone. She created jobs for herself at KSI, and she would be at the office until her eyes burned from too many hours staring at a computer monitor. She handled every odd job Brick, who had been left in charge in Tristin's absence, would give to her. She was getting to know the investigators well since she helped with research on the few cases trickling in. It still wasn't enough to stop the emptiness residing in her chest as she waited for Tristin to return.

It was crazy to feel this way for a man she'd only known a short time. She usually took her time dating a man, getting to know him slowly. It made a lot of sense to handle relationships that way. She could focus on her work without a serious commitment holding her back. If her relationship with the man went the distance, then she knew it was meant to be. Of course, she'd never had a relationship to go the distance, and now she was breaking her "take it slow" rule by sleeping with her boss.

To make matters worse, Tristin had been off the grid training for a few days with the Alpha Team, and she couldn't find relief from her doubts through their nightly phone calls. He told her that Jay's friend had a rugged wilderness training session planned for them, and they would not have cell phone service where they were. Jay's friend, Judah Cavanaugh, had a satellite phone, and Brick had the number should anything come up. Otherwise, Tristin and the team would be unreachable until Friday.

Kat was going crazy. She'd always been a loner, so she should be able to handle a few days by herself with no difficulty. But being alone meant she spent too much time doubting and imagining her idyllic world crashing around her.

Tonight, she couldn't handle another evening of questioning her future with Tristin. She invited the investigators over to dinner. Brick had quickly become like a big brother to her, and she was forming a friendship with Lex and Isobel she hoped would only grow stronger after an evening of good food and conversation.

She and Tristin explained her presence in his house by telling everyone she was house-sitting. She didn't think they were fooling anybody, but she felt less like she was taking advantage of Tristin by believing it was true.

With her favorite pop music streaming from an app on her new smart phone, she made quick work of dinner – a garden salad, homemade lasagna, fresh garlic bread and chocolate mousse for dessert. She hadn't cooked like this in a long time, and she had forgotten how much fun it could be. She just hoped the rest of the evening would be enjoyable, or her attempt to create a distraction would be in vain.

Kat had dinner well underway when someone knocked at the front door. With a smile, she smoothed her ponytail and adjusted her top before making her way to the living room. She had disabled the security alarm before she started dinner so the investigators could come straight through the gate without trouble. She threw open the door expecting to see one of them. Her smile died on her face.

"Who the hell are you?" The blonde's harsh tone took Kat off guard as much as seeing the strange woman on Tristin's doorstep. Her wide blue eyes were heavily outlined with dark shadow and eyeliner, and her full lips were painted a fiery red. She wore a black dress that clung to her curves like a second skin, exposing an ample amount of cleavage.

The woman breezed past her into the house before Kat could react.

"Since when did Tryst hire a housekeeper?" The woman circled the open space. "Just tell him I'm here and ready for a night of dancing at Torch."

"Ummm, and you are?" Kat asked.

"All he needs to know is that Amy is here. I promise, sweetheart. He'll be happy to see me."

The smug look on the woman's face had Kat struggling to keep a straight face. "Tristin isn't here, but I'll be sure to tell him you stopped by."

Amy's eyes narrowed. "Something funny?"

A giggle escaped, but Kat managed to contain herself. "No, not at all. I just was wondering why Tristin never mentioned you before."

The woman crossed her arms over her chest, pushing her ample breasts up and out. "You never told me who you are."

"It doesn't matter. I've already told you Tristin is not here, so you can be on your way."

"I don't believe you. I'll just look for myself." And Amy set off for the staircase as Kat called for her to stop.

"You have no business going up there." She heard another knock at the door. "Come in," she called as she hurried after Amy.

"Kat?" She recognized Brick's voice, and she looked over her shoulder to see him walk in with Lex and Isobel close behind.

She shouted down at him without slowing her pursuit of the blonde. "Hey, come with me. She won't leave."

Kat bounded up the stairs just in time to see Amy disappear into the master bedroom. Her humor dissolved into anger. She charged into the room until she stood toe-to-toe with the blonde. "I told you to leave. You have no business being in here."

"Sweetheart, I've probably spent more time in here than you ever thought about," the woman sneered.

"And how long ago was that?" Kat fired back. "I'm guessing it's been a while. Which is why you need to go. *Now.*"

"Who do you think you are? You have no right to throw me out. Tryst is not going to like this."

"I have every right because I live here. Now for the last time, get out!"

"Amy." From the proximity of his voice, Kat knew Brick stood directly behind her, but she never took her eyes off the other woman. "Tryst ended things with you a long time ago, and considering he's not here, he won't appreciate you being in his house. You need to leave."

"But she gets to stay?" Amy demanded, glaring pointedly at Kat.

"Yep. Tryst wants her here. He doesn't want you."

Amy took a menacing step toward Kat, but before she could

react, Brick placed his massive frame between the two women, protecting Kat from anything the other woman might do. Kat knew she could take the other woman. Brick's protective maneuver was unnecessary, but Kat was touched by the gesture. She glanced over her shoulder and saw Isobel and Lex moved to flank her and Brick, ready to step in if needed.

"Go, Amy," Brick ordered, his voice booming through the room. "Lex."

"On it." The other man grasped Amy's arm and led her out of the room, but not before the woman shot a look at Kat that would have rendered a lesser woman into a frightened puddle on the floor. Once Lex led her out of the room, Brick and Isobel turned their attention to Kat.

"*She* is the kind of woman Tristin dated?" she asked them, ignoring their stares of concern.

"What happened?" Isobel asked her.

"I opened the door thinking you guys had gotten here. She just barged in here wanting to see Tristin. She wouldn't believe me when I said he wasn't here. She didn't like it either when I said I lived here. God, is this what I have to look forward to being with him? Random women dropping by hoping for a booty call?"

"Booty call?" Isobel repeated. Kat's gaze locked with Isobel's dark one. A few seconds passed before they cracked grins. Kat saw the other woman, so mysterious and reserved, understood the absurdity of the situation she just experienced.

"She's gone," Lex announced as he returned to the room. "And Kat, I smelled smoke in the kitchen, and I took your pan out of the oven."

Her eyes grew wide as she gasped. "My lasagna!"

She bolted from the room back to the kitchen, drawing up short when she saw their dinner resting on the stove top, blackened and unrecognizable. She sighed and turned to see all her guests standing in the kitchen, staring at her.

"Sorry, guys. Looks like dinner is ruined."

Kat opened her mouth to say more but stopped. Her hand flew to her mouth as her eyes swept from Brick to Isobel to Lex. Before she could contain herself, laughter bubbled up from within her. It released as a giggle at first before erupting into a full belly laugh. She gave in to the hilarity of the evening until her laughter stole her breath and caused tears to stream down her face. She knew her guests probably thought she'd lost her mind, but at the moment she didn't care.

Brick and Lex exchanged puzzled looks, which only added to her mirth. Isobel grinned as she watched Kat.

"I'm sorry," Kat finally gasped. "I'm sorry. This is not how I thought this evening would go. I swear my life has more drama than a soap opera."

Her words brought grins to the men's faces and a chuckle from Isobel. She struggled to get herself under control before wiping the tears from her face.

"You okay, Kat?" Brick asked.

She nodded. "Yes, I'm fine. Thank you for all your help. I'm sorry dinner is ruined. We could order take-out, or if you guys would rather go, I understand. I'm sure you didn't expect to have to come to my rescue when you got here."

"If I go pick up dinner, will you explain to me what is going on? Because I'm kind of lost," Lex spoke up, causing a round of laughter from the others.

"I'll go with you," Brick offered. "I know this place nearby with the best burgers you ever sank your teeth into. It's no lasagna, but it'll work for a night of good company."

Kat smiled. "Sounds perfect. We'll just crash in the living room. Thank you."

Brick winked at her before dragging Lex by the arm. "Come on, Lex. I'll explain everything on the way."

The men left, and Kat glanced sheepishly at Isobel. Despite the background research on she'd conducted on the woman, the lovely investigator was still a mystery to her. No matter how many subtle attempts she made to encourage Isobel to share, the woman was a closed book. And now she had a ring-side seat to the drama that was Kat's life.

"I bought a bottle of wine to serve with dinner. Can I pour you a glass?"

"I'd rather take a beer if you have one," Isobel replied.

Kat moved to the refrigerator and withdrew two cold, long-neck bottles. She gestured for Isobel to proceed her to the living room. They settled on two overstuffed chairs where they could face each other. Isobel regarded her with emotionless, deep brown eyes. Kat finally broke the silence.

"I suppose you have some questions, too, about what went on tonight."

A slight smile curved Isobel's lips. "Questions? You mean like why did you tell her you were living here when everyone at work thinks you're just house-sitting while Tristin is gone? Or why you're concerned with more random women showing up to lay claim to the guy who's just your boss?"

Kat flushed. "Yeah. Those kinds of questions."

She had her suspicions Brick was aware of her relationship with Tristin though he had the good manners to never make insinuations about it. Because she'd been taken by surprise by Amy, she'd let her guard down, and too much information slipped out. There was no denying it now, but what was Tristin going to say when he found out she unveiled their little secret?

"Kat," Isobel pulled her out of her wayward thoughts. "I knew you and Tryst were together the first time I saw the two of you in the same room. And you can relax because no one thinks you're hooking up with the boss to climb up the ranks at work. Well, no one but the bitch who answers the phone and handles payroll."

Kat sat up straighter, her shock evident on her face. "Callie? She thinks I'm using Tristin? That woman never has liked me."

"I can't decide if she has a thing for Tryst or if she just doesn't like you coming on board and taking some of her power at the office. Either way I wouldn't trust her."

"I don't," Kat said, relaxing her posture once more. "She's not been very nice to me, and it was for that reason Tristin and I decided not to tell anyone about us. Especially since I'm still not sure what this is between us. Sorry. That's probably more than you wanted to know."

"So now that you've admitted to dating the boss, what about the woman who showed up here tonight?"

Kat giggled. "God, she was cliché, wasn't she? Since I've known him, I've seen no evidence of Tristin's reputation with women until Amy showed up here tonight, trying to stake a claim on him."

Isobel grinned. "Most women would have been jealous to have someone like her show up at her boyfriend's house."

"Boyfriend? I don't know about that or about being jealous either. I mean he either wants to be with me or he doesn't. The only thing I wonder about is after seeing Amy, if she's an example of the women he's been attracted to in the past, what could he possibly see in me?"

"Something better," Isobel responded, drawing a smile from her hostess.

"I hope he sees it the same way." Kat shifted into a more comfortable position. "What about you? Anyone special in your life?"

"Just Mo. My German Shepard."

"You don't open up to people, do you? It's Okay. I know it's none of my business. It's just I…"

Isobel raised a questioning brow. "Go on."

Kat flushed and lowered her eyes. "You fascinate me. You've done some awesome things with your life, and you seem like such a badass. I guess I'm just curious about you, but please know I don't mean to pry."

"I don't open up to people very much. Most women never know how to act around me because we usually don't have much in common. Most men are intimidated by me, and my career has never allowed me to build relationships with people. It's just me and Mo and my career. It's how I like it."

"I've always been a loner too. I have family, but my brother is a lot older than me. We were never close. He always acted like I was more of a nuisance than a sister. My dad died when I was young. My mother is the best, but she suffers from dementia now. I guess you could say I've been on my own for a while."

"I'm sorry," Isobel said softly. "About your mother."

"Thank you. But I don't want to focus on that. I want tonight to be fun. What do you like to do when you're not working?"

Isobel chuckled. "I don't do girl talk, Kat. I've never been good at it."

Kat grinned. "Well, then, help me choose a movie to watch then. Otherwise I'll be forced to have girl talk with Brick and Lex, and something tells me they aren't good at it either. We're going to need something to pass the time."

Kat handed Isobel the TV remote, and the woman flashed an answering grin as she flipped through the on-demand options for movies. When Kat's cell phone rang, she answered it without glancing to see who called.

"Kat? It's Brenda."

Kat's eyes widened. Her legs unfolded from underneath her, and her feet slammed to the floor. Why was her brother's wife calling her? Brenda was nice enough whenever Kat came to visit, but she never seemed interested in the two of them having any kind of close relationship. They had different priorities with Kat wanting to build her career and Brenda focusing on her family and social status. Kat knew Brenda gave a lot of her time to be with her mother while she was gone and Nick was working, and Kat respected the other woman for her dedication.

"Hi, Brenda. What's up? Is Nick okay?"

"Well, no, Kat, he's not all right. None of us are," Brenda answered gravely. "It's been a rough couple of days."

"What's happened?"

"Nick asked me to call you. He is…he is too distraught to talk right now."

"Brenda, please tell me. What's wrong?"

"It's your mother, Kat. She's very sick and in the hospital. The prognosis is not good, and the doctor says she may only have a day or two."

Brenda's voice wavered as she shared the news of Lori Walsh's condition. Kat froze, her body suddenly numb.

"I don't understand," she finally muttered, her head pounding.

"I know. It's all happened so fast. She's…she's asking for you. I believe she's holding on until you can get here."

Kat's heart shattered. A sob clogged her throat. "I'm coming. T-tell her to hold on. I'll be there."

A faint beep told her Brenda ended the call, but Kat sat as still as a statue, her phone to her ear. She felt an ache in her chest as her heart ripped in two. No tears fell from her eyes, and her sobs lodged in her throat. When she felt a warm hand reach for her phone, she jolted. She blinked to focus on Isobel, who knelt in front of her. Concern radiated from the other woman's eyes, but all Kat could dwell on was how warm Isobel's hands were on her own cold and clammy one.

"Kat, let me take the phone, okay?"

Kat simply lowered the phone from her ear and allowed Isobel to take it from her. Her hand remained outstretched, and she focused her eyes on it as if her palm was her lifeline. Isobel placed her phone on the coffee table before peering into Kat's face.

"Can you tell me what happened? I want to help."

Kat wanted to answer Isobel, but the words refused to form. All she could do was sit, unmoving, her childhood memories rolling through her head. Visions of her mother brushing her hair as they shared their secrets, of her standing in a chair at the kitchen counter while her mother instructed her on how to mix up chocolate chip cookies, and of her mother beaming as she opened her presents on Christmas morning.

Kat could hear voices muffled around her, but she was lost in the past, mourning what could be the end of her last semblance of family. Though Lori Walsh was a shell of the woman she once was, thanks to the dementia, Kat knew her mother loved her and was proud of her.

"Kat, it's Brick, sweetheart. You're scaring us. I need you to tell me what's going on. Do I need to call Tryst?"

Kat blinked rapidly, willing her vision to focus on her friend. She licked her dry lips. "I-It's my m-m-mother. S-she's d-dying. I h-have to g-g-go home. I h-have—"

And with that, the tears spilled from her eyes. Strong arms enveloped her, and Kat buried her face into Brick's chest. Sobs wracked her body as she gave into the grief consuming her. She was unaware of the plans being made around her.

"I'll pack a bag," Isobel said before disappearing into the master bedroom.

"She can't go alone, man. You need to call Tryst," Lex said quietly.

"He won't get back here in time, even if Wings flew them here. I'll go with her. Make sure she's okay."

"You sure, man? You're manning the company until Tryst gets back. I'm sure nothing's going to come up, but I'm not sure it's wise for both of you to be out of pocket just in case."

Brick nodded. "You're right. I'll ask Isobel to take her. I'll call Tryst once they hit the road. Give him a heads up."

Before Kat could even think straight, she was ushered into a car with Isobel behind the wheel, overnight bags stowed in the trunk. Other than providing directions to her hometown, Kat remained quiet as Isobel covered the distance in record time.

Chapter Twelve

Kat stood in the doorway, her feet frozen to the floor. The room was oddly bright, the fluorescent lights glaring against the beige walls. A monitor made its existence known with a persistent beep that grated on her nerves, and she curled her fingers into the denim covering her thighs. The acrid aroma of antiseptic mingled with a faint smell that made her think of urine, the scent causing her nose to wrinkle and her mouth to frown. Goose bumps rose on her arms as the cool air swirled from the ceiling vents into the room.

She was alone, save for her mother lying still in the hospital bed. She and Isobel had arrived to find only her sister-in-law in the waiting room. Brenda explained Nick had to make a phone call before the two of them went to her mother's bedside. Kat had asked for a few minutes alone, and Brenda had simply nodded before settling back into a chair to wait. Kat squeezed Isobel's hand to draw support from the strong, fearless woman before making the agonizing walk to the hospital room.

She wasn't sure what she expected, but the sight was enough to make her stomach churn. A blanket was pulled high, the top folded down at her mother's chest, which rose steadily. Lori Walsh's thin arms rested on top of the cover, her skin pale and smooth, her hands lined with age, her nails manicured short. Kat's eyes traveled up to study her mother's face, lovely and serene despite the oxygen tube at her nose. Her sable brown hair, limp and lifeless around her shoulders, still held a slight wave that left the ends curled in a subtle flip.

Kat wrapped her arms around her middle and propelled her feet forward. Isobel offered to accompany her to see Lori, but as much as Kat would appreciate the support, she wanted this time alone with her mother. Lori may not wake up or, if she did, even remember her, but that didn't stop her from wanting private time to say one last goodbye. Lori already knew the depth of her daughter's love for her. It was time she learned of the influence and wisdom she passed along as well.

Kat settled in a chair at Lori's bedside. She reached to grasp her mother's frail hand, her thumb stroking the top. She opened her mouth to pour out her heart, to make the most of what little time they had left together, but emotion clogged her throat, choking the words back. Tears flooded her eyes, and she blinked rapidly to keep them from falling.

"Oh, Momma," she finally whispered. She leaned forward to lightly kiss Lori's cheek. She already felt her mother's spirit seeping away from the bedridden body. Even if she could voice her thoughts and feelings, the words would be lost.

"I'll miss you. More than you'll ever know." She lay her head on the bed next to her mother's arm and allowed the sobs to overtake her.

"My Kitty Kat."

The voice was so faint she almost didn't hear it over the force of her sobs. Stunned, she looked up to see if she imagined the tender use of her childhood nickname, the one only used by her parents on rare occasions that made her feel special. Her sadness lightened when she met her mother's warm gaze. The dark pupils were clear, focused, and Kat's heart soared to know she would have one more lucid moment with the mother she remembered.

Kat swiped her tears away and smiled. "Momma. It's good to see you."

"Don't be sad, Kitty Kat. You will be fine. I'm proud of you. Your father would be proud of you. Of the woman you've become. So good, kind, smart. So much the woman I wanted to be."

"You're all those things, Momma. Where do you think I learned to be like that? From you and Dad."

Lori pulled her hand from Kat's grasp and rested the palm against her daughter's cheek. "I'm ready. I'm ready to see your father again. I've missed him."

The tears returned, and Kat didn't bother to stop them. Her chest constricted. "I'm not ready. I want more time."

"You don't need me, sweetheart. You have a life now. A full one, I suspect, since it's kept you from visiting."

"I'm sorry. I should have been here for you, Momma. I thought…I couldn't…"

Lori's hand fell weakly to the bed, but her smile was bright. "No apologies. No regrets. Tell me about this life. Are you happy?"

"Yes. I met someone. His name is Tristin. I work for him actually, and I probably shouldn't be…involved with him. But I can't seem to help myself. He's perfect. Supportive, funny, caring, handsome. You'd like him. I wish you could meet him."

"I felt the same way about your father. He was a rounder in his younger days. My parents called him a bad influence. I never wanted to disobey my parents. But Teddy would smile at me, tell me how pretty I was and how I made him want to be a better person, and I melted. Love happens the way it happens. No use fighting it, Kitty Kat."

"It could all disappear, Momma. I'm not sure I can handle that." She spoke of Tristin and so much more. Losing her father, losing her job, losing her home and now losing her mother. It was already too much to bear. If she lost him as well, she may never recover.

"You can handle anything. It's how we raised you."

Kat gave a strangled chuckle and planted another peck on her mother's cheek. "I love you."

"I love you, Kitty Kat. Now tell me more about this man of yours. I want to know him."

So, Kat talked. She told her mother about Tristin, about her job, about her co-workers who were also her friends and well on their way to becoming like family. She spoke of Tristin's home, which had become her home despite her best efforts to find something else. She spoke of Grayson Cove, of the diner with the best pastries she'd ever eaten, of the small shops that were locally owned and operated, of the friendly people she'd met who added to the quaint, welcoming town she'd come to love.

As the words poured from her, the tears spilled down her cheeks unchecked. She watched her mother's smile fade. She watched her lovely eyes close. She heard Lori Walsh's breathing even out. Through it all, she talked, barely registering what she was saying but afraid to stop.

Finally, Lori's chest stopped rising, her final breath leaving her body gently. The long, monotonic beep from the monitor signaled the end of a wonderful life for a wonderful woman.

Kat stopped talking, and her heart started breaking.

§

Kat stepped into the hall outside her mother's room after what felt like hours, but likely was only minutes. She wasn't sure. She didn't bother to check. Her tears marked the seconds ticking by as they streamed down her cheeks, dripping from her chin in a steady cascade of grief. Her chest felt broken like a chasm her heart had fallen into, the pain sifting through every pore until she was numb. Sadness warred with guilt to claim credit to the emptiness that consumed her.

"Kat?"

If her brother had used the harsh tone he reserved for conversations with her, she probably would have tuned him out. Instead Nick spoke with a softness that held a touch a fear, startling her to raise her eyes and fix them on his questioning face.

"S…she's…gone."

Kat choked out the two words before the sobs overtook her again. An arm wrapped around her shoulders and a hand settled on her elbow. She didn't look to see who it was because she only had one friend waiting for her – Isobel. She knew better than to expect support from the remainder of her family, which only made her grief more poignant.

After she settled in a chair, she watched through bloodshot eyes as Nick and Brenda clung to each other in a hug that was perhaps the most loving gesture she'd ever seen them show each other. She couldn't look away from the tears clinging to her brother's lashes. Nick wasn't an emotional person, and though she knew he loved their mother, she never expected such a public display of emotion from him. A kinship with him stirred, and she almost rose to offer her own comfort.

But before she could, he pushed Brenda away and whirled on Kat, desperation clouding his dark eyes. "How can you act like this wasn't exactly what you wanted to happen?"

A bucket of ice-cold water thrown in her face would have been less shocking to her system than her brother's accusation, laced with an ire she didn't understand.

"You think I wanted Momma to die? How can you say that to me?"

Isobel stood, stepping between her and Nick with a warrior stance. "I would tread carefully here, if I were you. You're crossing a line you can't come back from."

Nick ignored her with the ignorance of a man unaware of what the investigator was truly capable of.

"You have everybody fooled. Everybody but me. What did you think, Kat? That I would sit by while you took advantage of our mother this way? Did you think I wouldn't try to stop you?"

"Nick," Brenda coaxed from behind him, placing a hand on his shoulder to pull him back. "Now's not the time. You're making a scene."

"What are you talking about?" Kat rose and stepped around Isobel to face her brother eye-to-eye. "I've never taken advantage of our mother. I wouldn't do that."

"Deny it all you want," Nick spat at her. "It won't make a difference. I have proof. Don't think because Mother's dead that you're getting away with it."

"You're not making any sen---"

The arrival of two uniformed sheriff's deputies gave her pause. They looked to Nick, and after receiving a slight nod from her brother, they approached her. One – a short and stocky man with beady eyes and the face of a bulldog – waved a fold piece of paper at her as he spoke.

"Katarina Walsh, you're under arrest. Place your hands behind your head."

"Arrest!" Her heart slammed against her chest, her face becoming flushed with barely contained rage. She peered over the deputy's shoulder. "Nick, what did you do?"

"What are the charges?" Isobel demanded.

Under different circumstances, Kat would have been amused at how the deputies eyed Isobel warily. The second one – a handsome man of medium height and the slender build of an athlete – cleared his throat.

"Two counts of financial elder abuse," he explained as he pulled out his handcuffs.

"Abuse! But that's crazy. I only arrived in town today. How

could I have abused our mother? Nick, don't do this! We can talk this through and clear everything up. This is a mistake."

"The mistake is allowing you to have anything to do with our mother. She deserved so much better." Nick pierced her with a hard stare, and Kat could only return his look, aghast at what was happening.

"Deputies, there's been a mistake here," Isobel protested.

"Then it can be cleared up in court," said Deputy Bulldog. "Ma'am, I won't tell you again. Place your hands behind your head."

Kat's eyes darted from the deputies, to Nick, to Brenda, to Isobel and back again. Everything felt as if it was happening in slow motion, like a bad dream that wouldn't end.

"Kat. We'll get this straightened out. For now, just do what they say."

Kat whipped her head to stare at Isobel. "But I didn't do anything."

"I know. I believe you. But for now, this is what's best."

A sinking feeling sent her stomach falling to her feet. She realized Isobel was right. She had no choice but to comply until this mess could be sorted out and her name cleared. She nodded, resigned to her situation. She flattened her palms against the back of her head, and Deputy Handsome stepped behind her.

"You have the right to remain silent..."

He drew down one arm and then other before securing the handcuffs snugly to her wrists, all the while reciting her Miranda rights. She barely had the wherewithal to acknowledge her understanding of her rights before he placed a warm hand at her elbow to nudge her forward and Deputy Bulldog fell into step behind them.

As she moved passed her brother to the waiting room entry, she fixed her eyes on his face, now hardened in a mask of fury she didn't even know he was capable of.

"How could you hate me this much?"

"You never cared for her. Not like I did."

Another nudge from the officers forced Kat to move on before she could reply. She wasn't sure what she would have said anyway. She and Nick were never close, not in the way Tristin was with Travis or with any of the other Alpha Team members, who were just as much family to Tristin as his own blood relatives. But she and Nick had grown up together. They shared the same upbringing, shared the responsibility for their mother's care. He may not know what her hobbies were and how she liked her coffee, but she wanted to believe he knew her well enough to realize she would never do what she was accused of.

She propelled her feet down the hospital hallway, dropping her gaze to her feet so she could avoid the curious stares. The hushed whispers that followed in her wake were harder to ignore, and though she was innocent, she burned with shame. Her only solace was in knowing her mother would never learn of what her brother had done.

The Sheriff's Department cruiser was parked just outside the front doors to the hospital. She was nudged into the backseat, the car door slamming as if sealing her fate. Fresh tears pricked her eyes, but she blinked them away. Tristin, Isobel and the others wouldn't want her to show weakness. She felt that truth in her bones though there never was an occasion for them to voice those words to her.

Once the deputies settled in the front seat, Kat regained a fragile hold on her composure. As Deputy Bulldog pulled into the flow of traffic, Kat stared into the rearview mirror, hoping to communicate her innocence.

"I don't know what my brother had told you, but he's lying. I never abused my mother."

"You've the right to remain silent, remember? Well, that starts now." Officer Bulldog scowled at her reflection in the mirror.

Kat wished she'd had checked their name badges before they cuffed her. Using their names would show the respect she held for them and the job they did. It wasn't their fault her brother was out to get her. But she was forced to admit to herself any attempt to influence the two deputies would only fall on deaf ears.

She had no choice but to settle back against the seat as best as she could and await her fate at the hands of the judicial system.

Chapter Thirteen

During his military career, Tristin had been through all types of situations and conditions, many of which were undesirable. And yet he'd never been happier to reach civilization than when Judah Cavanaugh led them on foot into a clearing where cell service was restored. He fought a strong urge to drop to his knees and kiss the ground. Instead he double-timed it past Judah with the Alpha Team close on his heels, his destination being the headquarters for Judah's wilderness and training facility.

The time spent in isolation, with Judah running the Alpha Team through its paces, had served its purpose. The team members came together to operate as a unit much faster than Tristin expected, considering their diverse backgrounds and personalities. They still had some work to do to hone their skills as a team, but that would only improve with time and training. His chest puffed out with pride to see them working in tandem, each person's strengths utilized to benefit the whole.

But at the end of each training session, all he wanted to do was call Kat and share with her the progress they were making.

He'd been without contact with Kat or any of his staff for five days. He had formulated a plan to charm Judah's satellite phone away from him one evening so he could call Kat if for no other reason than to hear her voice. Fate had other plans when their first trek into the wilderness ended with Judah accidentally dropping the phone in a ravine, shattering their one source of communication. They debated whether or not to send a couple of men to headquarters for a replacement phone and finally decided it wasn't worth the time taken away from training.

Tristin never realized five days without talking with Kat would be such torture.

"Hey, boss. Why ya in such a hurry?" BB's pointed question prompted Tristin to roll his eyes and not respond. How the team had managed to pry out of him his plans for Kat, he'll never know. Since they sought every opportunity to tease him, he wished he'd kept it to himself.

"Leave him alone, B," Sam admonished. "If I had someone like Kat waiting for me, I'd be booking it back too."

Damn straight, Tristin thought with a grin. After having Kat in his house – and more specifically in his bed –he had no intention of letting her move into her own place. After leaving for the training trip, he recognized a need to connect with her, to be with her, to talk with her even if it was for a few minutes over the phone when he was too exhausted to hold his head up. It went beyond the sex. After five days of no contact with her whatsoever, he knew he was irrevocably in love with her.

As the Alpha Team fell into exhausted sleep each night, Tristin had lain awake, wondering about Kat's feelings for him. He wanted her in his life permanently, but would she be open to that? Did she care for him that much?

Each time his thoughts ran in this direction, he felt as whipped as his men teased him of being. He knew he was in trouble the moment he realized he didn't care about being whipped. He just wanted to talk to Kat. He needed to see her. Once he did, he felt certain he would know exactly how to proceed.

He stepped through the door to the wilderness headquarters and drew up short when he saw the grave expression on one of the employees' face. He met the man when they first arrived, but he'd forgotten his name since then. The reserved expression and then solemnness in the man's eyes set off Tristin's radar. Though the other man sought out Judah first, Tristin instinctually knew whatever bad news the man had was meant for him.

"Judah, I was just about to head out to find you. We couldn't raise you on the sat phone," the man began gruffly.

"It got busted on our first day. What's up?"

When the man shifted his eyes to stare at Tristin, he braced himself for what would come. "Mr. Knight, your folks have been trying to get in touch with you for two days. Your man Brick said to call him ASAP." The man handed Tristin his cell phone, which Judah collected and secured before they trekked into the wilderness.

"Tryst?" Jay spoke up as his boss started to walk off for a little privacy.

"Give me a minute," Tristin barked as he found Brick's name in his contacts.

Brick responded after only one ring. "Tryst. Where the hell have you been?"

"We just got back. What's wrong?"

"It's Kat, man. She's been arrested."

Tristin's blood ran cold as his mind spun in a million directions – from denial to doubt about how well he truly knew her to blind fury.

"If this is a joke, Brick, it's not funny," he deadpanned as he struggled to restore his control.

"No joke, man. You need to get there ASAP. The rest of the guys too. I have all of our resources on it, but we're being stonewalled."

"Shit! What do you mean 'there'? Where is 'there'? Look, have Callie call Jamie Rotherford. He's a corporate attorney who helped me and Travis set up our companies. See if he knows a criminal attorney who will take on Kat's case. Spare no expense-"

"Tryst, slow down. Travis has already arranged an attorney for her. Her name is Antonia Rollins, and she's the only reason we know as much as we do about what's going on. Isobel is running the investigation from Kat's hometown. That's where she was arrested. Lex and I have been handling things here. As far as Callie, well, I had to fire her."

"Are you shitting me right now, Brick? I'm gone for a week and all hell breaks loose! What the f---"

"Look, Tryst. I know you have questions, but there's no time to answer them all. You and the team need to get to Evergreen now. That's where Kat is. I've chartered you a plane waiting at Linder Airfield. It's the closest to where you are. Tell Wings a flight plan has already been filed, and I'm texting him the coordinates. Once you guys are in the air and Wings gives you the go ahead, call me back. I'll explain everything, but it'll take too long to do now."

Tristin only had more questions, but he willed himself to hold them in. His urge to get to Kat's side was greater than his need for information.

"Standby for my call. And Brick? Tell me she's Okay."

He sensed Brick's hesitation. "She's tough. One of the strongest women I know. She's hanging in there, but I imagine she's feeling pretty helpless right now."

"Shit!" Tristin muttered under his breath, running a hand through his hair. "Whatever it is, she couldn't have done what they're accusing her of."

"She didn't, man. She needs our help. She needs you."

Brick's words were just what Tristin needed to get his ass in gear. He quickly ended the call and turned to fill his team in on what little he learned. Instead he saw them heading out the door with their gear in tow, all except Wings, who regarded him intently with his beefy arms folded across his chest.

"Brick already texted me. I showed the team. Judah said the airfield is about twenty minutes down the road. He's calling ahead to have the plane ready, and we could be wheels up in less than thirty."

Tristin nodded stiffly before beating a hasty retreat out to the waiting SUV. He had a feeling the Alpha Team's training was about to be tested as they rushed to the aid of the woman their boss lost his heart to.

§

Kat could feel the tears welling in her eyes, but she refused to allow them to fall. She longed to succumb to her despair, to allow herself a good cry over how her life had turned completely upside down. But she was tired of crying, tired of how weak the tears made her feel. She had a target on her back, and she knew it. Any hope she had of escaping her prison had dwindled and all but disappeared. Her only recourse was to appear stronger and tougher than she felt.

She'd even pushed away all memories of Tristin. At first, they were all she had to carry her through the grief and pain she'd felt since her mother's death. After her arrest, she allowed the memories to comfort her.

Until she became lost in the past and didn't notice the other inmate sneaking up behind her. Before she knew it, the woman had punched her in the jaw and likely would have done worse if a second inmate hadn't stepped in to aid her. The other prisoners left her alone afterward, but she lived in fear she would be attacked again. Especially since her attorney delivered the disheartening news that her arraignment had been delayed until after the weekend.

She sat on her bunk, her knees pulled tightly to her chest. She heard her cell mate snoring softly in the bottom bunk, but sleep eluded Kat. The eerie noises she heard at the jail at night were enough to keep her awake. The betrayal she felt kept her company. She idly wondered when someone would visit her again, though the only people to have come were Isobel and her new attorney, Antonia something. She'd only spoken with the woman once, and that one meeting hadn't gone as she hoped.

She had been taken to a holding room after about an hour of being in police custody. Antonia was there, but what thrilled her more was to see Isobel with the attorney. Even though she knew the investigator wasn't an affectionate person, she pulled the woman into a tight embrace.

"Oh, my God. It's good to see you. I have no idea what's going on. They won't talk to me. I just—I just lost my mother. I should be helping with funeral arrangements, not sitting in jail."

Kat's moment of outrage was all she would get. Antonia had them sit down before she shared what information she'd gathered.

"The charges are financial elder abuse, Kat. It's not something I've dealt with before, and I'm treading new water here. Apparently, there's evidence you talked to your mother while she was battling dementia and convinced her to adjust her will to leave you the majority of her assets should she pass away." Antonia didn't mince words or attempt to sugarcoat her situation. Any other time, Kat would have appreciated the woman's straightforwardness. Instead she just wanted to hit the woman.

"That's bullshit! How can there be evidence? I haven't been home in months."

"That's what I'm trying to find out. Every time I've asked, they've stonewalled me. I need to know what I'm up against before they come in here to question you."

She released a sigh, a headache pounding behind her eyes. "Mom and I talked about her will once. It's been over a year ago. She said she didn't have much, but she would split it between me and Nick. She said she might make a small donation to her church. But she never mentioned anything else, and I didn't ask. I wouldn't talk about it with her for long because it was hard to think…" Kat's voice caught in her throat as tears welled in her eyes. She struggled for a moment to rein in her emotions. "It was hard to think of Mom being gone. The dementia was robbing her of her mind, but I was relieved we still had her, even if she didn't know who we were most of the time."

"Are you sure there's not more? They're holding you on two counts of financial abuse. Usually that kind of claim is tough to prove."

"Honestly, I don't know what they could have. I really don't. I don't understand what's going on at all."

Isobel leaned forward and held Kat's gaze. "We'll get to the bottom of it. I promise. I'll get in touch with Tristin and the team, and we'll take care of it. You have to hang in there. Let us do what we do best."

At the time, Kat believed Isobel to be speaking the truth. Now, in the darkness of her cell, she wondered how she would ever get her life back. Like her, Antonia and Isobel were certain Nick spearheaded the charges against her. She wished she knew where the supposed evidence originated from, but since she was stuck behind bars, she'd never be able to get herself out of this mess.

She should be angry, but she couldn't summon the energy to let the feeling materialize. She prayed for numbness to sink in, but she was lost in the pit of her grief. How much was one person supposed to endure? Just when her world started to turn around for the better, one phone call sent it crashing down around her.

One terrible phone call.

She'd replayed the call from Brenda over and over. Was there something in her sister-in-law's tone that should have alerted her to what awaited her at home? How could she not have realized her brother hated her so much that he would resort to this?

Kat didn't know when her mother's funeral was being held. For all she knew, it had already occurred, and she missed it. She wondered if that had been Nick's plan all along. What else could she derived from the fact he had two police detectives lying in wait for her the moment she left the hospital room? He resented her, probably from the moment he found out their mother was pregnant with her, which is why she could never bridge the gap between them.

The fact she underestimated his hatred of her cost her everything. She'd always managed to dig herself out of any horrible situation she found herself in. This time, her hands were tied, and she couldn't deal with knowing there was nothing she could do.

Chapter Fourteen

Tristin paced along the front of the courthouse, his fists shoved into his pants pockets. His heart pounded as he waited. If another minute went by without Kat walking out the front door, he'd race inside and find her himself.

The image of her cowered in a jail cell came close to sending him over the edge. He'd called in every favor he had coming to him and finally managed to turn the tables on the authorities in this Podunk town. No one had been cooperating with them since Kat was arrested, but he found a military contact who knew somebody who knew somebody who finally made things happen. Now he was waiting for Kat's arraignment to be over and for her to be released on bond.

Antonia had vetoed his presence in the courtroom, saying he'd only be a distraction Kat didn't need. He argued with the attorney until Isobel stepped in to agree with Antonia. Isobel had been hired as an official investigator for the defense, giving her a reason to assert herself in the case and be a presence in the courtroom.

Tristin couldn't wrap his mind around the whole situation. When he left for the Alpha Team's training retreat, he and Kat were happy. Their relationship was solid. He was ready to take it to the next level. How did they go from that to the love of his life sitting in jail for defrauding her own mother, who was no longer alive to defend her daughter's honor?

He froze in his tracks when he heard the courthouse doors open. His breath caught in his throat as he watched the very people he'd been waiting for emerge. Antonia and Isobel flanked Kat on either side, Antonia's hand at Kat's back to guide her steps. Tristin's gaze transfixed on Kat, noting the simple pale gray sheath dress skimming the delicate curves of her body, her signature braid falling over one shoulder, shining glittery bronze as the sunlight caressed the strands. Her eyes were downcast, her index finger rising to push her glasses higher on the bridge of her nose. Antonia spoke to her, but he wasn't sure Kat was listening. Tristin detected a green-yellow bruise marring her jawline.

Unable to wait any longer, his long strides carried him to meet the women halfway. Kat's head jerked up at his approach, her eyes widening as they landed on him. She stopped and moved to stand behind Antonia, as if the attorney was a shield protecting her – from what, Tristin didn't know. He opened his mouth to call to her.

Isobel moved in front of him, blocking him from reaching Kat. Antonia shifted her frame so she and Kat could move past him without him touching the woman he came to see.

"Kat!" His brow furrowed, fury blazing in the stare he turned toward Isobel. "What the hell?"

Isobel placed one hand on Tristin's chest while the other grabbed his bicep to hold him still. "She needs a minute, Okay? Antonia is taking her back to the hotel, and you'll get a chance to talk to her then. I know you're anxious to see her, but she's been through a lot. You have to respect her space."

He didn't like being kept from her, and he didn't entirely believe Isobel's explanation for why Kat avoided him. He realized Kat and Antonia had already made it to a car across the street and would be driving away before he could get to them. He would have to bide his time. Isobel and Brick had secured suites in one of the two hotels in town, and KSI had transformed them into a makeshift office where they could strategize. He would find a way to speak to her there.

"Come on," Isobel said, pulling his arm to propel him forward. "I'll catch a ride with you to the hotel, and we can talk on the way."

Isobel kept up with his quick strides to the SUV, and Tristin settled in the driver's seat. His hand gripped the steering wheel firmly, but he didn't reach for the push-start ignition right away.

"What the hell is going on?" He gritted his teeth as he stared out the windshield. If he looked at his investigator, he would lose what little control he had on his temper. He didn't know her very well, and the idea she was closer to Kat and her situation than he was made him crazy.

"How much do you know?"

He inhaled deeply and released it slowly. His finger depressed the ignition. "Just start at the beginning," he ordered as he shifted into drive.

"Kat invited Lex, Brick and me over to your house for dinner while you were gone. She was lonely and wanted to get to know us. She had to deal with one of your ex-lovers when we got there. The woman barged into your house, and we had to help escort her out. Kat handled it well, but later, before we ate, she got a call from her sister-in-law. Her mother was in the hospital, deathly ill. Brick didn't want her to drive here alone. Kat was in shock. So, I packed her a bag and drove her here myself. We arrived in time for her to sit by her mother's bedside before Mrs. Walsh died."

Tristin tensed, waiting for Isobel to continue.

"She walked out of her mother's room to the waiting room. I was there with her brother and sister-in-law. She was in tears when she told them their mother had died, and all hell broke loose. Her brother yelled at her, screaming it was all her fault, that she never cared for their mother like he did, and she only used their mother to get what she wanted. I started to intervene, but two cops showed up out of nowhere. Next thing I know, they were taking Kat out of the hospital in handcuffs. I tried to get to her, but they wouldn't let me see her. If they let her have a phone call, I don't know who she called because it wasn't any of us."

"You got her the attorney?

"I called Brick right away, but he was out with Lex on a case. I left a message with Callie."

"And Brick fired her."

"She deserved it. She has something against Kat. I knew it as soon as I saw them in the same room together. Callie never gave Brick my message. She even had Kat removed from the employment files at KSI when she found out Kat was arrested."

"Shit!" Tristin's outburst echoed throughout the SUV. "Why the hell would Callie do that? How much time was wasted before Brick knew what was going on?"

"A day. I tried finding Kat an attorney here, but I didn't trust any of them. She needed someone tough and smart who wouldn't buy into the rumors being spread about her, and none of the lawyers around here fit the description. Kat's brother knows a lot of people and has a lot of friends. Since I was having no luck with attorneys, I made arrangements for her to have protection from the other inmates."

Tristin whipped his head to stare at Isobel for a few seconds before turning his attention back to the road. "*What?* How?"

The woman shrugged. "It doesn't matter. I wasn't quick enough to keep her from getting punched by an inmate, but her protector stopped the fight before it got out of hand and made sure she was left alone from then on. I called KSI again, and your brother answered this time. He just happened to be there to check on things because Callie told him Kat abandoned her job. Callie had stepped away from her desk when Travis answered my call, otherwise I probably would never have gotten in touch with Brick at all. I explained to Travis what had happened, and he and Brick found Antonia. If anyone is going to win Kat's case, Tryst, it's Antonia. She's good, and she knows how to work the small-town politics we've been up against."

"Why are we getting resistance?"

"Kat's brother and his wife. Evidently, while Kat's been away, they've been dogging Kat to anyone who would listen. They've had most everyone of importance in this town believing she abandoned her mother and left her care up to Nick and his wife entirely. People have taken the lies and built them up to gossip about Kat abusing her mother and stealing from her family. Her reputation is shot around here."

Tristin pulled into the parking lot of the hotel. Killing the engine, he twisted in the seat to face Isobel.

"How is she? Why did she run from me?"

"She didn't run from you. She's overwhelmed, and the only people she's seen since this all happened besides inmates and cops are Antonia and me. If you could have seen her face when we told her you arranged for her to attend her mother's funeral, you would know her reaction has nothing to do with you."

He nodded. Finally out of questions to ask, he opened the door and stepped out. Isobel followed suit, and they moved side by side in silence. Once inside the hotel, they found the suite buzzing with activity. He saw Antonia gathered around a table with Jay, Sam and BB, pouring over papers scattered over the top. He didn't see Kat. Zane and Wings were also gone, but his girl was the only person he was concerned with. Isobel inserted herself into the conversation with the others, and Tristin wandered through the suite unnoticed.

The door to one of the bedrooms was ajar, and he peered inside to see Kat sitting on the edge of the bed. She stared unseeingly at the wall, so forlorn that his heart constricted. He slipped inside, but Kat didn't notice until he closed the door behind him with a soft click. She jumped to her feet, whirling around to face him. He stayed by the door though he yearned to be near her. He couldn't risk her running from him again.

"Hi," he said, wincing at how lame he sounded.

"Hi."

"I'm sorry, Katarina."

He watched her eyes pool with tears before she dropped her gaze. "Why would you be sorry? None of this is your fault."

He took a couple of steps closer to her then stopped. "I'm sorry I wasn't here for you. I told you I would be reachable if you needed me, and I wasn't. I swear I got here as soon as I knew what was happening, but it wasn't soon enough. You don't deserve any of this, and you certainly don't deserve to go through it alone."

Her hands opened and closed into tight fists. "I wasn't alone. Isobel and Antonia have been great. It's just…"

Her voice caught in her throat, and Tristin moved even closer. He could reach out to draw her to him, to wrap her in his arms and never let her go. But he refrained. Barely.

"It's not the same. You don't know Antonia and Isobel well, and while they've been nice to you, it's not the same as having someone who cares for you standing with you."

She raised her head slowly. Tears flowed unchecked down her cheeks, dripping from her chin. Her eyes were tortured, and Tristin's heart broke. "T-the only p-person who c-cared for m-me is g-gone. I c-can't believe it."

His resolve shattered. With lightening reflexes, he grasped her arms and drew her flush against him. One arm circled her waist while his other hand cradled her head against his chest. He felt the wet heat of her tears seeping into his shirt. He lowered his head to rest his lips against her hair, his eyes closing at the onslaught of emotion coursing through him.

"I'm sorry about your mother. I know you loved her very much, and I know without a doubt she loved you. I wish I could have known her. I wish I could have reassured her you are not alone. You have people who care for you. Since I can't tell her that, I'm telling you. You have a room full of people out there who will work tirelessly to prove your innocence because they care what happens to you. And you have a man in here who will move heaven and earth to protect you so you will always feel safe and always feel cared for. *Always*, Kat."

Her hands gripped the front of his shirt with a physical strength Tristin didn't know she possessed. Sobs raked her body as she clung to him. He never knew one person could shed so many tears, and he felt his chest tighten painfully to realize this much sorrow lived inside the woman he loved. He dropped butterfly kisses to her hair. He had no words to say to her to ease her grief, so he stayed quiet. If what she needed was to cry, then he would stand there the rest of his life if necessary and let her cry.

Several minutes passed before the last sob escaped her throat. Her shoulders stopped shaking, and she rested against him, completely spent. Tristin allowed himself a few more seconds to stroke her head, hoping she found some comfort in his awkward ministrations.

She didn't resist when he lifted her into his arms and carried her over to the bed. He settled her on the mattress and instructed her to raise her body up enough to draw down the duvet. Slipping her shoes off, he debated on finding something more comfortable than her courtroom dress to wear. Before he could make up his mind, she shifted to her side and curled into a ball, her hands folded together to rest on the pillow beside her head. He covered her to her shoulders, and her eyes slid closed. Tristin stayed by the bedside, watching her until her breathing evened out. Even once she was deep in slumber, he couldn't turn away.

He resolved right then she would not spend another night in jail. No matter what he had to do, he would protect her from enduring any more pain and humiliation.

He slipped quietly from the bedroom and made his way back to the common area. He was pleased to see all his team there, though Antonia had left. Conversation stopped as he approached, and his eyes met Jay's.

"How is she?"

"She's tough. She's resting right now." Tristin's face scowled as he swept his gaze to include his team. "I want this to end, so whatever it takes, we get to the bottom of this and prove she's innocent. She's not to spend one more day in jail."

"We're on it, but I got to be honest," Jay said. "It's not going to be easy."

"What have you found out?"

Sam spoke up. "Let me get Brick and Lex on the phone. They've been working this too."

Once the two investigators were on speaker phone, the rest of them settled around the folding table they borrowed from the hotel.

Jay started out the SitRep. "Nick Walsh, Kat's brother, filed the report with the police about what he called 'Kat's suspicious behavior.' He claims even though their mother was battling dementia, she would have moments of clarity, and some things she said during those moments raised red flags for him. According to the police report, he shared his concerns with the police but didn't file a formal complaint until his mother was hospitalized. That's when he discovered his mother's new will. He claims he knew nothing about it, but it leaves all his mother's assets to Kat and even grants her power of attorney with decisions regarding her mother's medical care and estate. Antonia finally obtained copies of the old and new will, and she said it all looks legit. The old will splits all the assets between Kat and Nick equally, but the new one cuts Nick out of it altogether. The new one even has Kat's signature on the witness line. We've tried locating the notary public who made it all official, but she apparently retired and went off the grid."

"How does this constitute fraud?" Tristin questioned.

"Because the date the will was signed and notarized was after Mrs. Walsh was admitted to the special care facility and deemed unfit to make decisions about her own affairs," Isobel explained. "There were also reports from the facility staff about how Mrs. Walsh would become agitated the few times Kat was able to visit. They never knew what she said to upset her mother, but the staff reported Mrs. Walsh was never agitated when Nick and his wife Brenda came to visit."

"Then there's the video," Brick's voice rang out through the speaker phone.

"Video?"

"There's a video at the local bank. Lex and I were able to secure it after Antonia told us about it. It's not the best angle, and the image is grainy. But it shows someone who resembles Kat going into the bank and transferring funds from her mother's account into a separate account in Kat's name. From what Nick told police, he used his mother's account to save funds to cover her expenses at the special care facility."

"And he never thought to report the theft before now?" Tristin asked incredulously.

"Nope," Lex piped in. "He never noticed it. His wife handles all the bills, and there was always enough in the account to cover the facility's monthly cost. The bank statements only showed withdrawals, not who was making them. The wife assumed the husband was making the withdrawals and never questioned him. And Nick was none the wiser."

"And Kat has no alibi for any of this," Isobel said. "She was in town on those dates, but she said she never went to the bank to inquire about a notary public nor to withdraw money. She would just visit her mom and then go back to her room at her brother's to work. She remembers her mother's agitation during some of her visits, but she never knew what caused them. The facility staff led her to believe it was part of the dementia, and sometimes they never knew what set her off. Kat thought little of it at the time. Even now, she has no explanation for any of it."

"Do we have any proof Kat didn't do this? Or even some way to explain away the evidence?" Tristin demanded.

"Not yet," Jay broke the news. "There was one date that threw up a red flag for me. It was a bank withdrawal made when Kat wasn't in town. She was on the road heading to Grayson Cove. The problem is there's no one who can verify her whereabouts. Because she stayed in her car and paid cash for her food, there's no record of her road trip or when she actually arrived in Grayson Cove. They can easily argue she had plenty of time to make the withdrawal and then make it out of town."

"This is bullshit!" Tristin exploded. "She would not do this! She is heartbroken over her mother. Her brother did nothing but make her feel guilty for not doing more to care for their mother. She was out of work for months, and she still tried to send him every dime she could to help with the expenses. The bastard is setting her up. I know it!"

Tristin no longer cared that his team knew private details of Kat's life. Right now, he needed them, and so did she.

"We know, Tryst," Sam interjected. "We just need to do some digging, but we'll figure this out. Kat's one of us. We've got her back."

Tristin took a moment to will his rage under control. "I know. Thank you. Thanks to all of you. I, uh… I just don't want to let her down."

"We get it, man," Brick added. "Neither do we."

"Tryst," Jay spoke up. "I think we need to go over the game plan for tomorrow. Kat is not a popular person in this town. Folks aren't going to be happy about the fact she's out of jail, much less seeing her at the church."

The church. For Mrs. Walsh's funeral. Tristin took a deep breath and released it slowly. "Brick, you and Lex work the investigation from there as much as you can. How's everything else going at the office?"

"It's fine. We've got it handled."

"Okay. Everyone else, work in shifts, but don't leave any stone unturned. We need this solved ASAP. Then come the funeral tomorrow, we all go. Kat needs all the support she can get, and I'm thinking we'll need to shield her from all the folks in this town who believe the worst about her. I don't get how one guy can turn a whole town against his own family."

"This guy and his wife are a piece of work. But we got this. We're going to figure this out," Jay vowed. "And we'll be there for Kat. No one's going to mess with her. We'll make sure of it."

Tristin nodded. He tried to tap down his frustration, but he couldn't stop his anger at how everything had shifted around him.

The future he envisioned with Kat was quickly fading away before his eyes.

Chapter Fifteen

Kat opened the bedroom door just enough to peer through and see if anyone else was up. The hour was early, just after sun-up, but she wouldn't be surprised to see any of her protectors wandering around the suite. They seemed to keep odd hours, especially since they started investigating the criminal charges against her. She appreciated their help and support, but she had something to do. And she had to do it alone.

When she didn't see or hear anything, she ventured out of the bedroom, stepping lightly. She slipped her purse strap on her shoulder and held her breath as she scurried across the room and slipped out the door of the suite. Her heart pounded, and she froze when the latch clicked as the door closed. Seconds ticked by before she could be sure she didn't wake anyone.

Her Uber waited for her at the curb in front of the hotel. She had been pleasantly surprised to secure the transportation so early in the morning, but she was grateful not to have to walk to her destination. She hoped to accomplish what she had to do before any of the Alpha Team or Tristin realized she was gone.

Her stomach clenched as the Uber drove up the drive to the long-care facility that was her mother's home. She hesitated when the car stopped at the entrance, fear warring with her nerves. The driver cleared his throat, and she smiled apologetically before stepping from the car. Taking a deep breath, she walked up the steps and through the front entrance.

The facility was quiet. A few of the residents were settled in the dining room as she walked by, and a handful of employees bustled around, completing their early-morning tasks. If any of them viewed her presence as unusual, no one said a word or paid her much heed. She walked with purposeful strides down a hallway to room one-twenty-one – her mother's room.

She placed her hand on the doorknob and twisted, preparing her heart for what she would find behind the door. Fortunately, all she found was an empty room. She worried the facility would have already cleaned the room of her mother's things and placed another resident in the room. She closed the door softly behind her and stood in the center of the room. She could feel Lori Walsh's presence around her, and she closed her eyes as grief flooded her anew.

Kat drew a shaky breath and proceeded to sort through her mother's things. She wasn't sure what she hunted for. She doubted there would be anything in the room to explain what was happening to her. Yet she needed to feel one last connection with her mother. She wanted to possess a memento to keep her mother's memory close. She doubted Nick would let her keep anything of her mother's possessions if she asked, so she was forced to just take it.

She walked over and fingered the knitted throw folded neatly and draped over the foot of the bed. The first time she saw her mother in this room, she had been lounging on the bed, covered with this throw Kat had not ever seen before, with a book open in her lap. Lori wasn't reading but staring off into space, and Kat watched her, feeling her slipping away to the effects of her disease.

"What are you doing in here?"

Kat whirled around to face the petite woman dressed in blue scrubs. She carried a couple of cardboard boxes, but she glared at Kat as if she was a militant police force and Kat was a criminal.

"I'm sorry." Kat held up her hands in a gesture of surrender, hoping to calm the nurse. "This was my mother's room. I just…It's the last place…I…" Her voice trailed off as words failed her.

The nurse's demeanor changed in an instant. She relaxed, her eyes regarding Kat with sympathy. "You're Mrs. Walsh's daughter. Oh, my, I'm so sorry for your loss. I meant to have her room packed up as you asked, but-"

"As I asked?"

"Well, the head nurse told me you called and asked for us to pack up her things. I completely understand. It's hard. But I didn't realize you would be coming by. I just assumed you asked us to do this so you wouldn't have to come back."

"It turns out I couldn't stay away."

"I can come back. You just take your time." The nurse was already opening the door.

"No, you don't have to go. Please, just do what you need to do. Is it okay if I help you?"

Kat could see she surprised the nurse, but the woman recovered quickly.

"Of course." She moved to place the boxes on the bed. "I'm sorry we've never met before. I work the late shift, and you are always here later in the day. Your mom was such a sweetheart. She talked about your visits all the time."

"My visits?"

"She looked forward to them. She said you would brush her hair and straighten her room. You would watch movies together. She was so proud of you."

Kat realized the nurse had mistaken her for Brenda, and she decided not to correct the woman's assumption. She wanted to hear more about her mother, and she couldn't risk the nurse realizing she was the one accused of manipulating her favorite patient.

Kat opened a drawer to get the packing started but paused when she saw her mother's nightgowns folded and stacked neatly. She touched the cool cotton and felt the tears prick her eyes. Then she saw another hand cover hers. She lifted her eyes to find the nurse beside her, smiling.

"Why don't you sit down, Miss Kat? Let me do this, and you can keep me company."

Kat nodded, suddenly exhausted. She settled in the pink recliner that came with each room and watched the nurse bustle around the room.

"What's your name?"

"Katie. Your mother used to tell me we would have to meet sometime, with our names being similar. Kat and Katie."

"It's nice to meet you, Katie. I appreciate all you and the rest of the doctors and nurses have done for my mother. I knew I didn't have to worry for her because she was getting the best care."

"That's sweet of you to say." Katie worked efficiently as she talked, and somehow her rhythm eased the flurry of Kat's emotions. "Your mother was precious. She was never any trouble and never wanted to 'put us out', as she called it. She would ask about us too. She always wanted to know how my husband and sons were doing. When my oldest had strep throat, she made a point to tell me that she prayed for him to get well. She told me how she had wanted to be a nurse when she was younger."

Kat nodded. "She would have been great, and my dad always encouraged her to pursue it. But they married out of high school, and she was pregnant with my brother before they were married a year. She decided spending time with her son meant more to her."

"Right, your brother. What's his name again?"

"Nick. But Mom would call him Nicholas."

"Yes, I remember now. She said he was serious even as a kid.

Other boys would be playing football outside, and Nicholas would be inside working math problems or reading a book. But you... She said you were full of adventure."

Kat laughed. "I don't know about that. I never was satisfied sitting still though. Not like Nick. Unless I was in front of a computer."

Katie joined her in laughter, and then the two fell into a companionable silence. Kat watched the nurse work and felt a peace settle over her. Though this wasn't the home she grew up in, she could feel her mother's warmth in this room. She cared for the people who cared for her, and Kat took solace in the comforting thought.

"I don't believe it, you know."

Kat shook her head to clear her thoughts. "I'm sorry. What?"

"What they're accusing you of. I heard about it, but I didn't believe it. No one who cares for your mother as you did would ever take advantage of her. She would be the first to set them all straight."

"Thank you." Kat studied the nurse as she worked, a sudden thought crossing her mind. "You know, I have to say I'm impressed you remembered my name and had trouble remembering Nick's. He's been taking care of Mom's expenses lately, and I just figured you all would know him better."

Katie shrugged. "He didn't come by to visit as much as you. I got used to seeing your name on the log-in roster when I would come in for my shift. And like I said, it was close to my own name."

Kat mulled over the nurse's words, something ringing false in what she said. As the fog started to clear and she pieced the information together, she realized she needed to get back to the hotel. Tristin and the team needed to hear what she learned.

"Katie, I'm sorry to leave you, but I think I need to go. It's-"

"I understand. It's a lot so soon after Mrs. Walsh's death. Don't you worry. I'll back everything up with great care. I'll leave it at the nurse's desk for you to pick up at your convenience. I am sorry for your loss. Your mother will be missed."

"Thank you. Do you think I could…take something with me?"

"Absolutely. And I think I know exactly what you want."

Katie opened a drawer in the nightstand and withdrew a red, leather-bound book. She handed it over with a smile. "Whenever she felt agitated, we could read to her from this book or even give it to her to hold. It always calmed her down. I think it's because it helped her feel connected to your father. She talked about him a lot too."

Kat ran a hand over the cover before opening the thin book of poetry to the title page. Emotion choked her as she recognized her father's familiar handwriting.

As Aristotle said, love is composed of a single soul inhabiting two bodies. You are the other half of my soul. You make me feel alive, and not a day goes by when I'm not overwhelmed with my love for you.

Kat never knew her father was a romantic. She wished she had asked her mother more about the book. She knew it was a birthday gift from her father, but she didn't know how he presented it to her mother or how her mother felt when she read the inscription. She had not thought of asking for the book to keep, but she realized Katie had chosen the perfect keepsake for her.

"Thank you, Katie. And thank you for taking care of my mom. It means a lot."

"You're welcome, Miss Kat. It was my honor."

Kat slipped out of the room and beat a hasty retreat from the facility. She couldn't risk anyone recognizing her and calling the police. As much as she wanted to check out the log-in sheet, she was pushing her luck the longer she stayed. She had to get to Tristin and get them to check out the log. Something wasn't right. She wasn't sure exactly what it was. She needed the experts to investigate it and help her sort it out.

She walked back to the hotel instead of calling an Uber. Needing the fresh air to clear her mind, she took a less traveled route to avoid stares from the people in town who recognized her. Her name was poison among the people she'd grown up around, thanks to Nick. More and more, she realized her life was no longer here. There wasn't anything tying her to Evergreen anymore.

§

Kat stepped back into the hotel room, lost in her thoughts. The door barely closed behind her before she was swept into a strong embrace. Her body was crushed against Tristin's, and her feet left the floor as he lifted her up to him.

"Oh my God! Where the hell have you been?" Tristin practically shouted at her while he squeezed the breath from her.

"Let me go, and I'll explain."

He loosened his hold, but he didn't let her go. "You scared the shit out of me. When I woke up and couldn't find you…"

"I'm sorry. There was something I needed to do, and I knew you would say no. I hoped to be back before I caused you worry."

"Why do you think I would say no? Anything you need, I want to be here for you."

"I went to see my mom's room. At the care facility."

Tristin stepped back, and Kat missed the feel of his arms around her. He was unshaven, his hair disheveled, but he looked perfect to her. She could feel his displeasure rolling off him, but she didn't care. As long as he was in her life, she could face anything – his frustration, her brother's hatred, and the terrible charges against her. Tristin was all she needed.

"Before you lecture me on what a bad idea that was, I need to talk to you and your team. It's important."

He peered into her face, searching her eyes for something. She wasn't sure what, but she allowed him to look.

"Are you all right?"

She smiled and reached out a hand to rest against his cheek. She loved the feel of the rough stubble against her palm.

"I'm fine. It was something I needed to do, and I don't regret it. I found something of my mother's that I can keep, something my father gave her. I have peace about her, but now it's time to end this attack my brother has launched against me. I think I have something that might help."

He grinned, and her heart melted to see the light in his eyes. "Then let's get the team together. I'm glad you're all right, sweetheart, but don't scare me like that again."

"I can't make any promises. But I promise not to shut you out again. I want you by my side, Tristin. I know you didn't ask for any of this, but I don't want to go through this with anyone else at my side."

"No place else I want to be. Come on. Let's get the team, and you can fill us in on what you found out. We were just about to head out to look for you."

He took her hand and let her into the suite, calling for the others to join them. She smiled at their enthusiasm to have her back safe and sound. She wished her mother could have met them. Not only would Lori love each of them, she would have been pleased her daughter found a new family to look over her.

"I went to see my mother's room at the long-term care facility. We sold our house when we moved Mom into the facility, so it was like her room was my last connection to her. Anyway, I was talking with one of the nurses who used to care for Mom. She works the night shift, and she was never there when any of us went to visit. But she knew me. She called me by name. She said Mom used to tell her about my visits and how she looked forward to them. She said she learned my name after seeing it on the log-in sheet," Kat explained. "It's what visitors have to sign when they come in for any reason."

"What does that have to do with your case?" Zane asked, never failing to surprise her whenever he chose to speak since it happened rarely.

"Maybe nothing. But she acted like she'd seen my name often enough that it stuck. Which doesn't make sense since I wasn't able to visit very often. The only one who did was my sister-in-law, Brenda. Nick didn't visit often either. The nurse didn't remember his name. And the nurse never asked me about Brenda. Just me. Don't you think that's odd?"

"It could be nothing. If your mother talked about you a lot, that could be the reason she remembered," Jay pointed out.

"And our names are similar. She's Katie, I'm Kat. But I don't know. Something felt off. I can't explain it."

"I'll check it out and talk to the nurse," Isobel volunteered. "If there's something going on, I'll find it."

"I'll go with you," BB spoke up. "This could be a lead."

Jay nodded. "Go. See what you can find out. But be back in time for the service. We go to the funeral as a unit."

As the group dispersed, Kat reached for Tristin's hand and squeezed it. "Thank you. I couldn't get through this without you. Without all of you."

"I'll always be here. No matter what. I've missed you, and when this is over, I plan on showing you just how much."

He dropped a light kiss to her lips, and she blushed furiously for the team to see the display. They all smiled but didn't say a word as they dispersed. Kat met Tristin's gaze, its intensity warming her.

"I can't wait." She just hoped the time would come for her to go home with Tristin instead of to a prison to never see him again.

Chapter Sixteen

Kat stood at the edge of the cemetery, clutching Tristin's hand and drawing strength from him. She sensed the presence of the others surrounding, taking their cues from her. As much as she appreciated their support, she wished they had allowed her to come alone because she had no idea what she should do next.

She thought today would be hard, saying goodbye to her mother again. But she was numb to the grief. She had no tears left to cry, and she couldn't bring herself to approach her mother's graveside.

Her thoughts were consumed with Lori Walsh, remembering her as a child remembers. In the winter when their house would have a chill, her mother would sit with her by the fire, combing through her freshly washed hair. Her mother would softly hum a nondescript tune and lull Kat into contentment. They rarely spoke in those moments. They just enjoyed each other's company.

She recalled the birthday cake her mother baked from scratch when Kat celebrated her sweet sixteen. Her school friends had elaborate parties with bakery cakes, but Kat thought the strawberry cake her mother made was much better.

She did want her last memory of her mother to be freshly dug dirt, the shiny surface of her mother's casket, and the sickening smell of the flowers Nick and Brenda chose. With the focus taken off her arrest and pending court date, it all melded together to make the loss of her mother more acute, more terrifying.

She had some time before the graveside service started, and no one questioned her need to stay on the periphery. Just a short time ago, they had arrived as a group to the church after the funeral had started and sat at the back. They left as the minister uttered the final prayer. Kat insisted on it so she wouldn't have to face the hatred and meanness of those who believed all the terrible charges against her.

The graveside service was closed to everyone but family, but she didn't expect Nick and Brenda to welcome her with open arms. She hoped to take advantage of the short time she had before they arrived, but she hadn't anticipated the moment to leave her too paralyzed to step into the cemetery.

"Katarina."

Tristin's voice was soft and comforting in her ear. She shifted her eyes to meet his, and he tilted his head to indicate a spot just over her shoulder. As she redirected her gaze, she felt her heart constrict when the hearse pulled up to the curb. She drew in a shaky breath, unconsciously squeezing Tristin's hand tighter.

"Are you ready, sweetheart?"

"No," she said flatly. "How can I do this? I can't say goodbye to her again. It hurt too much the first time."

"I know, sweetheart. I'm right here by your side. The minute it gets to be too much, you say the word, and we'll go."

She nodded. Activity behind her forced her to look back. The funeral home directors were opening the hearse's doors, and she went cold as the casket was pulled from the back. She wasn't how close her brother and his family were, but she barely gave them a passing thought as the casket was wheeled closer to where she stood. Her eyes followed it, her chest growing tighter the closer it came.

As the funeral home workers went by, the tears suddenly pooled in her eyes and fell in hot streams down her cheeks.

"Oh, Momma," she whispered on a sob.

An arm wrapped tightly around her shoulders, and she was drawn into Tristin's warm body. She drew in a deep breath, releasing it slowly. Her head dipped in a slight nod, and then she stepped from Tristin's embrace. She moved gradually on wooden legs, her eyes watching her feet. She felt Tristin's presence close behind her and instinctually knew the rest of her protectors followed as well.

Tristin's hand enclosed around her elbow, and she slowed her steps. She raised her eyes until her vision was consumed with the sight of the casket on the platform the funeral directors would use to lower her mother into the ground.

"Whatever you need, Katarina," Tristin murmured for her hearing only. "Just say the word."

Kat reached for his hand, and he quickly engulfed hers, squeezing it tightly. She didn't bother to wipe her tears away. One by one, she saw the Alpha Team step past her. They each carried a single yellow rose – her mother's favorite – and placed them on top of the casket. Kat had no idea where they found the roses or how they carried them without her noticing, but the gesture warmed her aching heart.

Tristin held a rose in front of her, and she accepted it with a watery smile. Together she and Tristin moved forward to place their flowers on top of the others. Kat rested her hand on the casket's smooth surface.

"Can I have a minute?"

"Of course," he responded, and she sensed rather than saw them all stepping away.

She drew curious glances from the funeral directors, and she could imagine what they were thinking. The daughter who is accused of taking advantage of her mother was now crying over her casket. She ignored them, knowing her time was limited, and she finally knew what she wanted to say.

“I know I wasn’t here for you like I should have been. I took for granted you’d always be there when I got my act together.” A hysterical giggle escaped her throat. “I even had visions of busting you out of that facility and bringing you to my new place. You would help me fix it up, and we’d live together like we were college roommates or something. Oh, Momma, I’m not sure how I’m supposed to do this without you. I didn’t care you couldn’t remember me sometimes. I still had you.”

She barely noticed her tears falling unchecked. “I wanted you to meet Tristin. And his team. But I’m glad I got to tell you about them, and you know I’m not alone. They’re like some band of brothers who have each other’s backs all the time. And for some reason, I’m part of it now. I don’t understand how it works yet, and right now it’s nice. I should be glad you aren’t here to see all that’s going on, but dammit, I wish you were here. I don’t know what to do, and you always seem to help me do the right thing.”

Kat lowered her head, her hair shielding her face. She willed her emotions under control. “I’ll miss you, Momma, but I’m glad you’re not hurting anymore. I love you, and I know you loved me more than I could ever know. Goodbye, Momma.”

She took a step backward and then another, her eyes never leaving her mother. “I love you,” she repeated.

Turning on her heel, she stepped forward only to draw up short. “Oh!” she cried, stunned to find her sister-in-law in front of her.

Brenda was a tall, slender woman with mousy brown hair, thin lips and wide eyes now dark with unreadable emotion. Kat never had a loving relationship with her sister-in-law, but she’d never seen the woman appear so forlorn either. Brenda always seemed self-assured and capable, unflappable by anything life could throw her way. Kat knew with her brother’s demanding job and with her having to search for work, Brenda was left to shoulder the responsibilities of her mother's care.

Brenda never attempted to build a friendship with Kat, and Kat always felt her sister-in-law cared only for the kind of life Nick's professional life could provide than truly being a part of their family. Kat never made much of an effort either, preferring to be alone when she wasn't with her mother. Despite their rocky relationship, Kat's heart ached for the woman, understanding how much Brenda must be hurting with the loss of Lori Walsh.

"You shouldn't be here, Kat," Brenda said softly enough for Kat to have to strain to hear her. "You'll just make this more difficult."

"I was just leaving, I promise. I just needed a minute."

Her sister-in-law nodded. Her thin arms crossed across her chest and stepped to the side to let Kat pass. As she moved to leave, Kat couldn't help but notice how pale Brenda appeared. Kat paused, her eyes searching Brenda's face.

"Should I get Nick for you?"

The other woman's eyes widened frantically. "Oh, no! Please don't. I'll be fine. He got a phone call just as we got here, but he won't be too much longer. Please, just go. It's for the best."

"Brenda, I've never told you, but thank you. I appreciate all you did for Momma, and I know she appreciated it too. As much as I wanted to be here, I'm glad you were there for her when I couldn't be."

Unshed tears shimmered in Brenda's eyes, and she lowered her head.

"Your mother never knew who I was most of the time. After one of your visits, she would call me Kat for days. When she did remember, she would ask me how you were and when you would be coming back. I think she preferred you to be with her instead of me."

Kat reached out to lightly touch Brenda's forearm, but when the woman jerked away, she dropped her arm to her side. "You're wrong. When I visited her, she would tell me all about your visits. How you would brush her hair or bring her favorite cobbler or show her photos of your kids. She said she knew how busy you and Nick were, but she was glad you found time to spend with her. I was actually a little jealous to be honest. You were spending the kind of time with Momma I wish I could."

A sob broke free, and Brenda buried her face in her hands. Kat noticed her nephews standing nearby, alerted to their mother's upset. When they moved to come to Brenda's aide, Kat smiled weakly at them and waved to reassure them their mother was going to be fine. Kat wondered if she should hug Brenda, but she hesitated since they didn't have that kind of relationship.

"I'm so sorry. I know you loved Momma, and she loved you too. I didn't mean to upset you. I really didn't. I…" Kat sighed, realizing nothing she did would improve the situation. "I'm going to go and leave you and Nick in peace. I just…I just want you to know I didn't take advantage of Momma. I didn't do the things I'm accused of. I would never try to cheat her or you and Nick."

Kat's words made Brenda cry harder. Kat opened her mouth only to close it as words failed her. She didn't know how to comfort her sister-in-law, but she suddenly didn't feel right leaving Brenda alone when she was this upset.

"What is going on here?" Nick's voice blasted Kat as he appeared at Brenda's side.

Kat stepped back, her eyes sweeping the cemetery. Tristin and the others were alerted by Nick's shout and started advancing toward them. Nick wrapped his wife in his arms.

Kat wrapped her arms around her as if to protect herself from her brother's wrath. "Nick. I swear I didn't-"

"Haven't you done enough to tear our family apart? Why are you even here, Kat? Leave or I'm calling the police!"

"I was only trying to help."

"By upsetting my wife? Leave! If you continue to harass us, I'll see to it you get put away for a long time."

Tristin was almost to her side, but she waved him away as she faced her brother. "I didn't do anything to our mother. I swear I didn't."

"The evidence suggests otherwise."

"I didn't, Nick. I would never—"

"Shut up, Kat. Leave now, or I'm calling the police. I need to bury my mother. I don't have time to deal with you."

"Hey, man." Tristin inserted himself between the two siblings. "You need to back off. She's not causing any trouble here. She just came to say goodbye to her mother."

"Not causing trouble? You could have fooled me."

Brenda suddenly pulled from her husband's embrace. Mascara lines streaked her cheeks, giving her face a ghastlier appearance. "Nick, stop. You have to stop."

"Brenda, go sit with the boys. I'll take care of this."

"No. You need to listen to me. You have to stop. Please."

"Brenda, I know you're upset-"

"Listen to me for once in your life," Brenda shouted through her tears. "You need to stop because you're wrong. You've always been wrong."

"Brenda, now's not the time."

Brenda jerked her arm from her husband's grasp. "It never is. You never have time for me. If you did, none of this would have happened. It's all a lie, and you can't even see it."

It's all a lie. Brenda's tone was detached, as if she was addressing strangers. Something about her words stirred Kat's suspicions.

"Brenda, what's a lie? What are you talking about?"

Kat didn't expect her sister-in-law to answer her, so when Brenda pierced her with a hard stare, she instinctually took a step back.

"I'm not sorry, you know. You ran away, and it was left up to me. All of it. If you had been here, nothing would have changed."

"Don't talk to her." Nick squared off against Kat. "You need to leave. You don't belong here."

"What does she mean? I'm not leaving until I know. What was the lie? What changed? What is she talking about?"

"Can't you see she's overcome with grief? She stayed with Mother and cared for her when you weren't around. They became very close. She deserves to grieve in peace. She was more of a daughter to Mother than you ever were."

Kat gasped as the heat of her brother's words sliced her heart. "How dare you! How can you say that?"

"Lori never liked me." Her sister-in-law's admission effectively ceased the siblings' back-and-forth.

"You're talking nonsense, Brenda. What's gotten into you?" Nick hissed.

"I'm tired. Of all of it. I'm tired of the secrets, of the stress, of the judgment. It's a mess, and you won't listen to me. You never listen to me."

"I'm listening," Kat spoke up. "Tell me what's wrong, Brenda. I only want to help you."

"You don't want to help me. Not when you find out what I did. Please go. You're just making it worse."

"For the love of God, Brenda, shut up!" Nick snapped. "We're leaving."

Nick grabbed his wife's arm, this time holding tight enough so she couldn't struggle free. He dragged her toward the folding chairs where their sons waited and watched the display.

"What did you do?" Kat called after Brenda.

"She framed you. She's the one who committed fraud against your mother."

Isobel's voice was strong and clear, carrying over the serene cemetery like a vocal steamroller. All eyes turned toward the investigator, including Nick and Brenda's. Isobel regarded them all as if she was privy to all the secrets surrounding the small group. That's when Kat noticed her friend held her phone in front of her though her eyes zeroed in on Nick and Brenda.

"Don't be absurd!" Nick's face flushed a deep purple as he blustered. "If you don't leave, I'll have you arrested too. Maybe you can share a cell with my sister."

Brenda slipped her arm from her husband's clutch. She backed away, her eyes wide and frantic. The truth dawned on Kat even before her sister-in-law spoke to Isobel in horror.

"No! No, no, no. How did you know?"

Chapter Seventeen

Brenda Walsh's four little words rocked the group standing in the small cemetery. They forgot about the funeral directors waiting somewhat impatiently for the family to assemble at the graveside. They only gaped at the regal woman looking like a lost little girl who had just been caught stealing a piece of candy from a store.

Brenda approached Isobel, and the investigator stood her ground even as her colleagues readied for potential trouble. Brenda stared at Isobel as if she was under a microscope, a puzzle that was meant to be solved. Seconds ticked by as the group tried to process what was unfolding in front of them.

"You figured it out, didn't you? But how?" Brenda's voice held a touch of wonder even as she paled and began to wring her hands.

"You're not a criminal. I just followed the trail you left, but I wasn't completely sure until just now."

Brenda nodded at Isobel's explanation, and Kat gasped as the truth settled into her psyche. Before she could question her sister-in-law, Nick positioned himself between Brenda and Isobel, and his wife had no choice but to face him directly.

"Don't say anymore. We're leaving."

"You may as well let her talk, Mr. Walsh," Isobel interrupted. "Once we go to the police with the results of our investigation, the truth will come out. And I believe Mrs. Walsh would like to ease her conscience."

Brenda shook her head and wrapped her arms around her middle as if to ward out what was happening.

"Brenda…"

"Nick, please, don't. There's no way you can understand."

"Tell me it isn't true. Tell me she doesn't know what she's talking about."

Kat felt like an intruder, witnessing the private moment between her brother and sister-in-law. She sensed the foundation of their marriage cracking under the pressure of the truth, but she couldn't look away.

"I can't do that," Brenda admitted. "She's right. Your sister is innocent. It's a lie. All of the evidence is false."

"What are you talking about?"

"I did it. The will. The bank account. The insurance policy." Brenda pointed to Isobel, who stepped to the side, her phone trained on the couple. "She's right. The truth was bound to come out. I got away with it for so long I thought I didn't have to worry. I never thought you'd involve the police or that you'd have Kat arrested. Once an investigation started, I knew it was a matter of time."

"You forged my mother's signature to a new will?" Kat interjected. "Why would you do that to me?"

Brenda sighed as fresh tears welled up in her eyes. "I didn't forge anything. Your mother signed it during one of those confusing moments when she thought I was you."

"I think you need to answer her question," Tristin said, his tone ice cold. "Why would you do that?"

Nick rounded on him, wild-eyed. "She doesn't owe any of you an explanation. She's distraught and doesn't know what she's saying!"

"Stop, Nick," Brenda admonished. "They know, and I might as well explain."

"No—"

Brenda held up a hand to stop her husband. "Please, Nick. Let me finish. You owe me that. Then you can take me to see our lawyer." She moved away from Nick and faced Kat as she explained. "I never meant for any of this to get out of hand. I'm not sure what came over me. I was overwhelmed and tired and…frustrated. I missed the way my life used to be. I know that's no excuse, and there's no way I can make you understand."

"Why don't you start at the beginning?" Kat tapped her anger down, needing to hear Brenda's confession more than she needed to lash out.

"You already know the beginning. You left. You sold the house, and you left. You realize all the talk of putting your mother in the facility for her own health and wellbeing was a lie, don't you? Nick convinced you to agree to put her there because he didn't know how to cope with caring for your mother. Lori hated the facility, you know. She wouldn't tell you or Nick – I'm not sure why – but she told me. Whenever she had a lucid moment, she would rant and yell at me about how she hated it and how she wanted to go home and how hurt she was that you two sold her house. I almost stopped going to visit, but Nick told me it was important. Since he works all the time and you were gone, he left me to handle it all.

"She could be obstinate sometimes. She had moments where nothing satisfied her, and she would get angry. You probably don't believe that since the Lori you remembered was kind and unassuming. She changed while you were gone. The staff said it was the dementia that made her so difficult at times. I knew they must be right, but it didn't make it any easier to deal with."

"Why didn't you tell me?" Nick demanded.

Brenda sighed. "You never wanted to talk about her. You just wanted me to say I handled whatever the problem was, and then you wouldn't have to be bothered. I didn't mind the difficult times so much. She would listen to me when I tried to calm her down. I wish it was because she respected me, but honestly, it was because she wouldn't remember who I was. She called me Kat more than she used my real name. She talked about how much she treasured Kat's visits and how precious Kat was to care for her and to put her life on hold for her." Brenda pierced Kat with a heated glare. "Only it wasn't you who visited or cared for her. It was me. It was always me."

"I never meant for you to shoulder that burden alone," Kat said.

"But you weren't here to stop it." Brenda buried her face in her hands and drew a shaky breath before facing everyone again. "When you did visit, it just made things worse. She would get agitated when you left and started complaining again about wanting to go home. I started pretending I was you. The dementia made it easy to confuse her into believing me. She was easier to handle when she thought I was you. I figured what harm was it actually causing?"

"How did you go from that to framing Kat for fraud?" Tristin pushed for the confession.

"That was never my intention. It all just sort of…happened. During one of her confused moments, she started talking about her will, how she left everything to Nick and Kat. But she wished she had just left it all to Kat because her daughter came to visit while her son didn't. Kat was getting all the praise for the things I was doing. I couldn't help it. I got angry. I needed to vent to someone. I needed someone to agree with me and to recognize all that I did. I confided to a friend of mine, and she made an innocent comment. 'Too bad your mother-in-law can't change the will.'"

Brenda faced Kat as she continued. "Suddenly changing the will was all I could think about. Why should you get anything when I did all the work? I didn't start out with any intention of framing you for anything. I swear that never crossed my mind. But I knew if Lori believed it was what you wanted, she would rewrite the will, giving me your share of the estate. Then I would have my own resources and wouldn't have to rely on Nick any longer."

"None of this makes sense," Kat said.

"I know. It got all messed up. I pretended to be you when I brought up changing the will. I really thought Lori would go along with it because in her eyes, you could do no wrong. I didn't expect Lori to get upset about it. She was angry I would even suggest writing you out of the will. I dropped it because I realized the dementia distorted her reasoning. I thought the matter was over, but I didn't realize Lori believed Nick put you – or me posing as you – up to tricking her to change the will. Another resident helped her draft the new will, cutting Nick completely out as payback for him trying to manipulate her."

"But that can't be legal," Nick sputtered.

"The new will was never filed, and with her dementia, no, it's not legal," Isobel explained. "But that didn't stop you or the DA's office from filing charges against Kat for fraud."

"The date of the will is the same date as one of Kat's visits," he argued.

"A nurse told me my signature was on the visitor's log, but I wasn't here on some of the dates on the log," Kat added.

Brenda sighed. "That was me. When I started pretending to be Kat, I didn't want one of the nurses checking the log and figure out what I was doing. I forged Kat's name. I started changing my appearance a bit when I visited alone, so if Nick came with me, none of the nurses would put two and two together. He would only visit in the evenings anyway, which usually is a different shift of nurses, but I didn't want to risk anyone finding out what I was doing."

"I don't understand. Why would you make everyone believe I tried to cheat my family?"

"Nick found the will in her room at the facility and made the assumption. I decided not to correct him because I thought we could use it to contest the actual will and have a judge rule in our favor. I never thought he'd file criminal charges."

"Why let it go so far? You posed as me to clean out the bank account for Momma. And what is this about an insurance policy?"

"Some stupid insurance policy the facility takes out on the patients. We had to name a beneficiary, and I put myself. It was just easier than trying to get you and Nick to agree. And the account…I needed the money. In case I had to leave town. I couldn't risk people at the bank mentioning it to Nick, and I pretended to be you and made sure I used a teller I'd never met before."

"I never realized you hated me that much."

"I don't. I know you have no reason to believe me, but it's true. I resented you, moving away to live your life the way you wanted. I felt like my life was slipping away. Between taking care of my husband and sons and then your mother, there was nothing left. I don't expect you to understand. I'm not sure I understand myself."

"Oh, Brenda," Nick muttered. He turned away, running his hands through his hair.

Brenda rushed forward, gripping Nick's arm. "Sweetheart, please, I know what I did was terrible, but you have to forgive me. I was desperate."

"His forgiveness is the least of your worries," Tristin exploded, startling Kat with his intensity. "You set Kat up to spend years in prison for something you did! What the hell? Jay, call the cops. We're turning her ass in and getting Kat exonerated."

"Tryst," Kat spoke to him calmly. "Please, don't."

He glared at her incredulously. "Kat, you've got to be kidding. She framed you for taking advantage of your mother. You went through hell because of her."

"You're not sending my wife to jail."

Kat shifted her attention to Nick. He still stood away from Brenda, as if he was too angry to touch her, but the ire burning in his eyes was meant for Tristin and her.

"Dude," BB piped up. "Your wife committed a crime and almost sent an innocent woman to jail. She's going to prison."

"We'll talk to our lawyer, Nick. We can work this out. Maybe I can get community service or something," Brenda said. "I'm a wife and mother. I can't go away. Who will take care of my family? I acted out of an extremely stressful situation. The judge will understand. Please, Nick, don't leave me to deal with this alone. Not again."

"I'm sorry I wasn't here, Brenda, but you have to know Momma appreciated you," Kat told her. "She may not have had the presence of mind to tell you, but she told me. She said you were the best thing to happen to my brother."

Fresh tears leaked from Brenda's eyes. "No one told me."

"That's no excuse for what you've done," Tristin snapped. "You are going to straighten this out and clear Kat's name. She shouldn't pay for something she didn't do. You've made her an outcast in this town."

Nick clenched and unclenched his fists. "There's no proof my wife did anything. She's distraught and overwhelmed. She wasn't thinking clearly."

"She confessed," Jay interjected.

"It's your word against hers, and we are well-known in this town. You are nobody," Nick said coldly.

"Nick," Kat returned. "This isn't right. I know I haven't been here for you like I should, but I don't deserve this. You know I don't deserve this."

"She's my wife! The mother of my children," Nick shouted. "You want to rip her away from her family? No! I won't let you."

"You don't have a choice." Isobel moved forward, holding her cell phone in front of her like a trophy. "I recorded everything. All we have to do is show this to the prosecutor, and the charges against Kat will be dropped."

Nick growled before lunging for Isobel, but Wings and Sam stepped up to shield her. Nick retreated, but his face reddened with unreleased rage. Brenda approached him slowly.

"Nick, I'm sorry. I never meant for any of this to happen."

Kat stepped away from Tristin to regard her brother and sister-in-law. "Momma wouldn't want this, any of it. We should be saying goodbye to her right now."

Nick's eyes slid closed as he worked to regain his control. His head tilted in a jerky nod before he opened his eyes, gripped Brenda's elbow, and moved to stand with his sons. He signaled the minister to begin the service. Kat could only imagine what the man must be thinking of their family drama.

"What do you want to do?" Tristin murmured in her ear. "Do you want to stay?"

She shook her head. "No. I said my goodbyes. I just want this day to be over. I can hardly take it in."

"I'll call the police and fill them in on what we know. We'll make sure Nick and Brenda don't slip away before the cops can talk to them," Jay said.

"They're not going anywhere." Fatigue laced Kat's tone as she watched the small family at her mother's graveside. "They have nowhere to run to. Nick won't leave his life behind like that."

Tristin drew her close to his side. "Come on, sweetheart. Let me get you out of here. The team has a lot to do, but you and I are going to hide from the world for a little while."

Kat couldn't imagine how this nightmare would play out, but

the idea of escaping with the man she loved was a temptation she couldn't resist. Tristin led her out of the cemetery, their friends and teammates falling into step behind them.

Chapter Eighteen

The sun rose emitting brilliant strands of orange and gold, but its beauty was lost on the young woman tormenting herself with what-ifs. Kat crossed her arms over her middle, oblivious to the chill in the morning air. Leaving the warmth and security of Tristin's arms had been a struggle, but her churning thoughts drove her from the bed. She didn't want her restlessness to wake him from a sound slumber.

She fought the urge to look at her phone screen for a missed call or text she already knew wasn't there. She'd spent the last six weeks anticipating a communication from her brother, but her attempts to reach out went unanswered. She wanted to mend the rift between them, to move toward restoring their family. Nick was stubborn, but Kat could handle stubborn. Working with the alpha males at KSI had honed that particular skill set. Her mother would have wanted that for her children. She was right in trying to build a relationship with Nick.

But Nick wasn't interested. The message she received last night confirmed that, even though a part of her still held out hope. His three-word response cut her to the quick: "*Leave us alone.*"

She hoped he might regret his decision. Part of her anticipated an apology text waiting for her each time she looked at her phone. But despite her best efforts and her heartfelt words, she had been rejected. Anger had her cursing under her breath. She was the victim, so where did Nick get off shutting her out? His wife set her up to be arrested, and she still took the high road by trying to repair their fractured relationship. Nick spent years making her feel like a worthless, immature loser, and she still sought a connection with the only family she had left. Who did he think he was to deny her that?

Then her mother's voice whispered to her heart in the same gentle way Lori Walsh went through life. Her mother saw the good in every person and every situation, even under the worst circumstances. She always encouraged her children to look beyond someone's rude behavior to find the motivation beneath.

"You never know what heartache someone is experiencing. You could be the kindness they need to turn their life around." The mantra fueled every decision her mother made. It affected how she parented her children. Kat never bought into her mother's belief, and now she struggled with her mother's words haunting her. She was the victim, but it was the reminder of her mother than had her empathizing with her brother.

Nick believed he was more of a parent to her than a sibling, and she fought him every step of the way. She shouldn't be surprised he was blaming her for how things turned out. Antonia turned over the video from Isobel's phone to the judge and the prosecutor. Kat made one final appearance in court before the charges were officially dropped. Tristin ushered her out of town soon after, and it was another day before she learned of Brenda's arrest.

With Antonia's help, Kat talked with the prosecutor about leniency for her sister-in-law. Kat didn't understand Brenda's motivation to do what she did, but she couldn't ignore the care and love her sister-in-law showed her mother. She wanted to hire Antonia to represent Brenda, but Nick refused, paying for an attorney on his own. She had a difficult time explaining her reasoning to Tristin, who couldn't understand her desire to connect with people who'd hurt her so badly.

Kat was grateful to return to her home in Grayson Cove. She

wasn't sure exactly when she started to regard Tristin's house as home, but after her time in jail and the turmoil of her mother's death, Tristin's fortress was exactly where she wanted to be.

Her life resumed. She stopped looking for her own apartment since Tristin had no problem with her staying with him. She went back to work and began drafting procedures for how she would assist the Alpha Team on cases. Back from their training, the guys were eager to roll out on a case. Tristin shared with her he thought that day could come sooner rather than later. She wanted to be ready when it did.

"Hey, beautiful." Tristin slid his arms around her waist and drew her into his body. His chin rested on her shoulder.

Kat placed her hands on top of Tristin's where they rested on her stomach. "Hey. Sleep well?"

"Better than you, I'm guessing," he growled into her ear, sending a shiver down her spine. "You all right?"

Kat sighed, once again absorbing strength from the man she loved. "I think so. It's just a hard pill to swallow."

"Your brother again?"

"I finally heard back from him. A text ordering me to leave them alone. I'm done, Tristin. I can't keep trying to win someone over who wants nothing to do with me."

Tristin turned her around in his arms until she looked him in the eye. "Maybe he just needs time, baby. You've tried. The ball's in his court now. If he decides not to be in your life, it's his loss. I, for one, am glad to have you in mine."

Kat smiled. She melted into his embrace, her head resting against his chest where his heartbeat thundered in her ear. Tristin tightened his hold on her. He buried his face in her soft hair and breathed in the scent that was her signature.

"I love you, Katarina," he breathed against her hair.

Her heart pounded a staccato against her chest. Since they'd returned to Grayson Cove, they had danced around their feelings for each other. Tristin showed her a million different ways every day how he felt about her, but neither had voiced their feelings aloud. Until now.

When she raised her head, her feelings radiated in her eyes. "That's the first time you said that to me."

"I should have said it before because I've known for a while. I love you, Kat."

"I love you, too."

His shit-eating grin split his face. A giggle escaped her mouth a moment before Tristin's head descended. He captured her lips, his tongue plundering her mouth. A moan rumbled up from within her as fire lit her body. Her hands wandered up his arms until her fingers tangled in his hair. She molded her body to his, loving the delicious feel of him against her. The searing kiss stole her breath. She could feel herself getting lightheaded, but she didn't want the kiss to end.

Tristin released her mouth only to drop heated kisses to her cheek, her jawline and down her neck, to the sensitive spot at her collarbone left bare by the vee neck of her shirt.

"Say it again, Kat," he moaned as he continued dropping kisses to her skin. "I need to hear you say it again."

His voice was ragged and knowing she did that to him only fueled her desire. She placed her hands on either side of his face, raising it until she could stare into his eyes. The irises had darkened to a smoky blue. She knew his eyes only appeared that color when he was turned on. It was becoming her favorite color.

"I love you, Tristin. More than I thought possible. I never expected it. I never expected you. But oh, my God, am I glad to have you."

His smile mesmerized her. She expected him to return her expression of love. Instead, he hoisted her effortlessly in his arms, eliciting a squeal from her. He cradled her to his chest, and her arms circled his neck. He carried her through his house back to the bedroom and tossed her to the rumpled sheets. Her laugh echoed through the quietness as she sank into the mattress.

Tristin loomed above her. His gaze roamed from the tip of her head, where her hair splayed across his pillows, to her toes, which started to wiggle under the intensity of his scrutiny. He knelt beside the bed at her feet. With a wolfish smile, he captured one of her toes in his mouth, sucking the digit until Kat was gasping from the sensations shooting up her body. Then his mouth trailed up her legs, lingered at her knees so his tongue could lave at the ticklish skin at the back. When he reached the apex of her thighs, Kat's breath caught in her throat.

"Tristin," she breathed as his tongue seduced her. Heat exploded within her, and the sensations overwhelmed her. She clenched the covers as moans erupted from her throat.

His fingers joined his mouth in taking her to new heights of pleasure. Just when she thought she might die from the ecstasy building inside, her orgasm shattered her. Tristin continued to use his fingers to drive her higher as she rode the orgasm until she was nothing but a boneless mass on his bed.

"Tristin," she gasped.

He crawled up the bed until he stretched his body along the length of hers. He kissed her, a gentle, leisurely caress of his lips against hers.

"I love you," he whispered against her lips. "And now I'm going to make love to you until we forget everything but the two of us."

She smiled serenely. "So, what are you waiting for?"

§

Peace.

Living his life the way he did, seeing the things he's seen, Tristin wasn't sure peace existed.

Looking over his backyard, at his friends and loved ones gathered, laughing and talking smack to each other, he knew peace.

The barbecue was just what he pictured when he thought of today. The fall weather warmed enough to make temperature comfortable, perfect for the outdoor gathering. His brother was quick to help with the plans once Tristin shared the idea with him. He watched the faces of his employees whom he counted as friends and who quickly were becoming family.

His Alpha Team – Jay, BB, Wings, Sam and Zane – were all different, but they were cementing together just as he pictured. Brick, Lex and Isobel surpassed his expectations with their capabilities and their dedication to the company. They all welcomed Kat as part of their team. His dreams for Knight Security and Investigations were coming true.

Tonight, his dreams for his life would as well.

Jay and Sam manned the grill while everyone drank beer and told tall tales. Tristin walked to the patio table. He reached over the back of the Kat's chair to grasp her hand. Then he pulled her to her feet to stand beside him. His arm draped over her shoulders, drawing her close to his body. He could feel her curious stare as he drew the attention of their guests.

"I'm glad to see everyone having fun. It made me decide that now is the perfect time to add to that." He turned to face Kat, grinning at the bewilderment furrowing her brow. He grasped her hand and dropped to one knee.

Catcalls and cheers went up as Kat's free hand covered her mouth. His heart melted in his chest.

"Katarina Walsh, you blew into my life like a force to be reckoned with, and I have never been the same since," he began.

"Thank God for that!" Travis piped up, eliciting laughter from everyone but Tristin, who sent a good-natured glare at his brother.

"Just ignore him," Tristin told Kat. "What I'm trying to say is I never understood what my life was missing until I met you. You've been by my side while I built my company. I promise you to be by your side for anything, for everything, for the rest of my life. I love you, Katarina Walsh. Will you marry me?"

Tristin pulled a velvet box from his jeans pocket and opened it to reveal the diamond ring he custom-ordered for her.

Kat smiled as tears welled up in her eyes. She nodded her head slowly at first, and then emphatically as she responded. "Yes. Yes, I will marry you."

With a shout of excitement, Tristin rose in one fluid motion and pulled Kat flush against him as he crushed her mouth with a long, heated kiss. Applause and cheers went up among his friends when he slipped the ring on her finger, pleased to see it was a perfect fit. Soon the newly engaged couple were surrounded, delighting in well wishes and hugs.

"Congratulations, you guys," Jay said. "Kat, I, for one, am glad to see my friend settling down with a strong, beautiful woman such as yourself. It means more women for the rest of us." He grinned as laughter flowed from the group. "This is a celebration, guys. The burgers and dogs are off the grill, so let's eat!"

Soon, the friends sat around the patio table, their stomachs full and their hearts content. Tristin squeezed Kat's hand, and she sent him a smile.

"Thank you," she murmured loud enough for only him to hear.

"For what?"

"For today. It's been perfect. For taking a chance on me by giving me a job. For supporting me through all that's happened. For all of it, Tristin. I love you, and, well, thank you."

"My pleasure, baby. It's just the beginning for us."

His cell phone interrupted the intimate moment. Tristin withdrew it from his pocket without releasing Kat's hand. Once he saw who called, he stood, motioning to her that he needed to answer. He moved away from the group for quiet and privacy. The call lasted only a few minutes. When it ended, he stared at the cell resting in the palm of his hand. His heart pounded.

He shook his head to restore his focus before returning to the group. Once they saw the seriousness of his expression, they grew quiet. Anticipation dripped from the air.

"Alpha Team, we have our first case. Go, pack up your stuff, and meet at KSI within the hour. I'll brief you, and then you're heading out."

The group sat in stunned silence. He could understand their reaction. He couldn't believe they had a case, and he couldn't believe it was a case that, resolved successfully, could solidify the reputation of his company and the team.

With a wide grin, he said, "What are you guys waiting for? This is it! Move your asses!"

A second ticked by before Jay stood. "You heard him. Roll out."

And just like that, the team rushed to their vehicles parked in the drive. Kat stood to start cleaning up when Isobel stopped her.

"Go. Brick, Lex and I have got this. The team needs you too."

Tristin grabbed his fiancé's hand. "She's right, babe. You're part of the team. Time is critical on this case, and we need to go."

As they hurried to Tristin's truck to head out to Knight Security and Investigations, Tristin admitted he agreed with Kat's assessment of the day. From starting the morning showing her how much he loved her, then getting engaged, and taking on his company's first special ops case, the day had indeed been perfect.

Author's Note

Thank you for taking the time to read Knight's Haven. This book was my debut into the publishing world, a dream I've had since I was a teenager. I loved writing Tristin and Kat's story, and I hope you loved it as well..

If you enjoyed Knight's Haven, please consider leaving a review on any or all of these platforms: Amazon, Goodreads and Bookbub.

For the latest updates on my books and upcoming book signings, sign up for my newsletter at www.shelleyjustice.com.

About This Author

Shelley Justice is a Southern belle who lives with her husband and two children in Alabama. Her love for the written word inspired her to start writing when she was thirteen years old, and she's been living in her imagination and crafting stories ever since. In addition to being a bookworm, she is a self-proclaimed TV addict with a special affinity for dramas. She also loves romantic movies, especially of the black-and-white variety.

www.shelleyjustice.com
https://linktr.ee/authorshelleyjustice

Acknowledgment

I have to thank my husband and my two daughters – Ricky, Ally and Delaney - for their love and their support. None of us knew where this journey would take me, and I couldn't have pursued this new venture without your encouragement. Whether or not you understood why I would get excited over the smallest milestones, you joined me in celebrating. I love you all and am so thankful for you each and every day.

I thank my best friend, Christie, for her constant support and demand to read my stories. For every time inspiration hit, and you sat back without interrupting while I wrote my ideas down before I forgot them. For all the times we talked character traits, book titles and plot twists like we were discussing our latest book obsession. You are the best!

Then to the crew of beta readers whom I also call friends – Susan, Shondae, Christie - I thank you for your honest and kind feedback and your encouragement. To my writing sisters – Emily, Colleen and Maryann – thank you seems inadequate when I think of all the ways you've helped me on this journey. Your friendship and mentorship mean more to me than I could ever tell you.

More From This Author

Read more from Author
SHELLEY JUSTICE

KNIGHTS OF KSI SERIES

Available on Amazon
Read for Free with Kindle Unlimited

KNIGHT'S HAVEN
Book One

KNIGHT'S RESCUE
Book Two

KNIGHT'S TEMPTATION
Book Three

KNIGHT'S JOURNEY
Book Four

KNIGHT'S HOLIDAY
Book Five

KNIGHT'S DESIRE
Book Six

KNIGHT'S FALL
Book Seven

KNIGHT'S SEDUCTION

Book Eight

KNIGHT'S HONOR

Book Nine

Meet the

LEGENDS OF FIRE CREEK

They were once wayward boys until they were taken under the wing of the original Legend. They grew under his tutelage to become vigilantes who look after those who aren't able to help themselves. They are loners thrown together in an unconventional family, living with secrets that shaped them into the men they've become. None of them know the meaning of the word normal, but they've known no other way. Until they meet the women who show them what it means to be loved and accepted for who they are.

Available on Amazon
Read for Free on Kindle Unlimited

Legends: Jackson
Book One

Legends: Luke
Book Two

Legends: Easton
Book Three

Legends: Ben
Book Four

www.ingramcontent.com/pod-product-compliance
Lightning Source LLC
La Vergne TN
LVHW010700110826
845149LV00014B/3181